W9-BVW-346

"You're burned here too," Max ground out, pressing a finger to her shoulder and, with one more look into her eyes, he dropped his head and pressed a kiss there, his lips searing her skin.

Paige trembled.

"Am I?" She bit into her lip. "Anywhere else?"

He moved behind her, his finger trailing a line across her back, between her shoulders, then his lips followed its path, pressing kiss after kiss to her skin until goose bumps covered her body. "Here." Then he kissed her other shoulder, but this time, it wasn't a quick, light kiss, but rather a caress, and rather than lifting his lips, he glided them higher, to the pulse point at the base of her neck, which he flicked with his tongue, his warm breath, his mouth, until she was so awash with pleasure it was almost impossible to stand.

"Max." Her voice emerged as a tortured whisper, for surely this level of desire *was* a torture device?

Brooding Billionaire Brothers

Passionate, commanding, irresistible!

Billionaire half brothers Luca Cavallaro and Max Stone may have had very different childhoods, but blood is thicker than water. These powerful men are much more alike than they want to admit—apart from being infamous in the business world for their ruthlessness, their ice-cold hearts are also completely untouchable! That is, until they meet the only women to thaw them...

The Sicilian's Deal for "I Do"

Luca Cavallaro may have left Mia Marini at the altar twelve months earlier, but she's haunted his dreams ever since...and now he wants to claim her for the wedding night they never had!

Contracted and Claimed by the Boss

Paige Cooper was looking to escape her celebrity status, not run straight into a contract that could bind her forever to brooding billionaire Max Stone...

Both available now!

Contracted and Claimed by the Boss

CLARE CONNELLY

If you purchased this book without a cover you should be aware that this book is stolen property. It was reported as "unsold and destroyed" to the publisher, and neither the author nor the publisher has received any payment for this "stripped book."

HARLEQUIN®
PRESENTS™

Recycling programs
for this product may
not exist in your area.

ISBN-13: 978-1-335-59338-2

Contracted and Claimed by the Boss

Copyright © 2024 by Clare Connelly

All rights reserved. No part of this book may be used or reproduced in any manner whatsoever without written permission except in the case of brief quotations embodied in critical articles and reviews.

This is a work of fiction. Names, characters, places and incidents are either the product of the author's imagination or are used fictitiously. Any resemblance to actual persons, living or dead, businesses, companies, events or locales is entirely coincidental.

For questions and comments about the quality of this book, please contact us at CustomerService@Harlequin.com.

TM and ® are trademarks of Harlequin Enterprises ULC.

Harlequin Enterprises ULC
22 Adelaide St. West, 41st Floor
Toronto, Ontario M5H 4E3, Canada
www.Harlequin.com

Printed in Lithuania

MIX
Paper | Supporting
responsible forestry
FSC® C021394

Clare Connelly was raised in small-town Australia among a family of avid readers. She spent much of her childhood up a tree, Harlequin book in hand. Clare is married to her own real-life hero, and they live in a bungalow near the sea with their two children. She is frequently found staring into space—a surefire sign she is in the world of her characters. She has a penchant for French food and ice-cold champagne, and Harlequin novels continue to be her favorite-ever books. Writing for Harlequin Presents is a long-held dream. Clare can be contacted via clareconnelly.com or on her Facebook page.

Books by Clare Connelly

Harlequin Presents

Emergency Marriage to the Greek
Pregnant Princess in Manhattan
The Boss's Forbidden Assistant
Twelve Nights in the Prince's Bed

Brooding Billionaire Brothers
The Sicilian's Deal for "I Do"

Passionately Ever After...
Cinderella in the Billionaire's Castle

The Long-Lost Cortéz Brothers
The Secret She Must Tell the Spaniard
Desert King's Forbidden Temptation

Visit the Author Profile page
at Harlequin.com for more titles.

PROLOGUE

AT NIGHT, when she slept, Max always checked on his daughter, then flicked out the neon-pink and purple lava lamp that adorned her bedside table, but not before he'd lingered a moment and studied her restful features. Lately, it had brought him a strange clutch of pain, because in sleep it was easy to believe she was the same little girl—gentle and funny—that she'd always been, until the last few months. Now, her temper was so quick to flare, her moods so unpredictable, there were times in the day when he barely recognised his Amanda.

But at night, he stood at her bedside and focused everything he had on her, willing her to return to a state of happiness, to be settled and content. Most of all, he hoped she understood how much he loved her.

His own childhood had made it difficult to express that love, but God knew he'd tried. Showing affection of any kind didn't come easily to the reclusive billionaire, but that didn't mean he didn't feel it.

He wanted, most of all, to be better. Different. A far more active and involved father than his own had been, and his own mother, too. When it came to parenting, he used them as examples of what *not* to do, and until recently that approach had served him well.

But just as the seasons sometimes shifted without being noticed, so too had Amanda changed without Max's being fully cognisant of it, at first. Little tantrums had been easily ignored—he'd even found them amusing initially. But the storm had kept building, and shifted from the horizon to the homestead, so he could barely remember the last time he'd had a conversation with his daughter that hadn't ended in raised voices—usually hers but, to his shame, sometimes his.

Max had always been a success.

As a boy, he'd been the fastest, the smartest, the best and brightest, his natural competitive instincts stoked to a fever pitch by parents who always withheld their praise even when it was the thing he most badly wanted. While his motivations had changed—he no longer cared for anyone's approval nor praise—he was no less determined to succeed in all aspects of his life.

Under Max's guidance, the family's luxury holdings business, which included his personal project—the pearl farms here in Australia—had gone from a respected yet boutique business to a global powerhouse, their various brands, be that jewellery or handbags or clothing, recognised the world over. That success was gratifying, but his primary focus was always Amanda. Succeeding at being a good parent was what mattered above everything else to him.

If the proof of the pudding was in the eating, then at the moment he was failing abysmally. Though it went against every grain in Max's body to admit it, and he absolutely hated the necessity of what he was compelled to do, there was nothing for it. For the first time in Max's life he needed help, and for Amanda's sake he would damn well make sure he got it.

CHAPTER ONE

IT WAS UNLIKE anything she'd ever seen. Still stiff from the long journey halfway across the world, and a little air sick from the shorter flight to the top end of Australia in a small, private aeroplane, Paige Cooper felt her eyes fill with red dust, but even through that orange haze she could still see, and she was mesmerised. A long way from the airstrip, the road was just a track cut through the desert, lined with sparse trees populated with about a million cockatoos, majestic against the afternoon sunlight. But as she went, the sleek black four-wheel drive bumping across unseen potholes and rocks, the trees thickened, grew greener, the air became darker as the canopy formed overhead, lustrous and sweet-smelling—mangoes, and something else, something indefinably tropical.

The road, which had been straight for miles and miles, began to weave, to twist and turn, each bend revealing more thick forest and tiny patches of blue sky, until there came a final bend and the ocean of Wattle Bay hit her in the face, glittering like a blanket of diamonds, turquoise, so beautiful, better than a postcard, and quite unlike anything she could have conceived of existing in real life. She thought of everything she'd left behind all those years ago in LA, the beach she'd come to associate with a life she would rather forget and parental mistreatment that had permanently shaped and sculptured Paige's outlook on life, but this beach was different. It was more elemental, somehow. There were no high-rises here, no tourist shops. It was just white sand, crystal-clear water, so many trees it took her breath away.

The house itself was also completely different from what she'd expected. After all, the Stones were, Paige knew, one of the wealthiest families in the world, their high-end jewellery stores synonymous with luxury and wealth. Paige had even worn one of their diamond necklaces to the first glamorous awards ceremony she'd attended. Paige had been only twelve, but her mother had insisted she 'look older' and had chosen a revealing dress, sky-high heels and expensive jewellery—despite her success that night, Paige couldn't think of it without a sinking feeling in the pit of her stomach, just like any of the times she'd been pushed by her parents into situations that had made her skin crawl.

What Paige hadn't realised until accepting this job was that the Stone family empire had all started with pearl harvesting, that way back in the early twentieth century, they'd begun to cultivate south sea pearls, and that this property in the far north of Australia was their biggest operation.

So it wasn't unreasonable for Paige to have expected some sort of modern, LA-esque testament to wealth, a showpiece home with miles of glass and visible ostentation dripping from every surface, but what she saw was, in many ways, the complete opposite. Her eyes, a shade of green almost identical to the tropical trees growing rampant overhead, skimmed the house and something like pleasure tugged at her heart—a pleasure she hadn't expected to feel here in the wilderness of the world.

Or was it perhaps relief? She'd been running on instinct for the last month, since the announcement had been made about her parents' tell-all book and Paige had broken out in a clammy sweat. Would she never be free of them? Despite having legally divorced them in her teens, the ghosts of her manipulative mother and father still haunted her. All Paige had wanted was to pretend the book wasn't happening, but, sure enough, interview requests had found their way to her, paparazzi had even showed up near the school of one of her charges. With her cover blown, Paige had known she needed to flee to a new assignment, ideally as far from civilisation as possible.

Staring at the house, she took in the details without allowing her heart to respond, even when it was difficult to ignore the charms of this property. But Paige was resolutely unaffected: she was always hired for short-term roles—at her own insistence—and an essential part of what she did was provide help without getting emotionally attached to people or property.

There was a large area of neatly manicured lawn, signalling a small claim of man's dominance over the abandon of this forested area, but the house seemed determined to surrender itself back to nature. It was made all of timber, except for the windows, of which there were many, and Paige's first thought was that it was a tree house for grown-ups. It stood three stories high, but it was charming rather than grandiose, from the outside at least, with weatherboard painted a pale cream, a large wrap-around balcony on which, from her vantage point, Paige could just make out a day bed and table. She immediately pictured how nice it would be to sit on one of the cane chairs with a cup of iced tea and stare out at the view.

But she wasn't here to relax. This was work—and she understood she'd have her hands full.

The agency who'd recruited Paige had warned her that the house was quite isolated, and so she'd expected silence— a silence her soul desperately needed after the din in her personal life over the last four weeks—only this was anything but! The birdsong was incredible, a true orchestra of nature, humming, buzzing, carolling all around her, so she had no choice but to stop and simply listen, to pay respect to the beauty of this land and its animal inhabitants, to allow herself to be enchanted by the wonder of it all.

And that was how he found her: Paige Cooper—pale, pearl-like skin luminescent in the afternoon sun, her large eyes transfixed, red lips parted, auburn hair pulled over one shoulder in a concession to the stifling humidity, unconsciously seeking a hint of ocean breeze against the skin of her neck, small, slender frame, in that moment of unguardedness, projecting a hint of the fragility she'd worked so hard to conquer over the years.

Max Stone stopped, mid-step, took one look at the woman the agency had sent and had to stifle a groan. Because while he knew he needed help, he'd fought against that necessity ever since placing the call to arrange a nanny.

Max hated the idea of having someone else living under his roof, taking ownership, in a strange kind of way, of his daughter. It made him feel like a failure. Worse, it made him feel like his own father, who'd outsourced whatever parts of Max's life he possibly could, only taking an interest when it became clear Max had a head for business that would make Carrick Stone's life easier.

He hadn't given much thought to the nanny as a person, certainly not as a woman, but as he stared at the slim person in the middle of the lawn, something inside Max ignited that brought his body to a grinding halt. He stood perfectly still and stared at her, inexplicably angry to find that she was beautiful and attractive—for he'd known many women who were the former without being the latter—and he didn't need the complication of desiring the woman he'd hired to care for his daughter.

He should send her away immediately, ask for someone else.

Only, he was truly desperate, and she was reported to be the best. Besides, this was only a three-month assignment, she was here temporarily. Besides, Max hadn't been with a woman in a long time, and he had no intention of giving into temptation now, just because she'd be living under his roof. He formed one hand into a fist at his side, forced himself to focus.

'Paige Cooper?' His voice was gruff, and her eyes flared a little at the roughness to his words. The churning in his gut intensified. He ground his teeth, squared his shoulders then channelled every last inch of his legendary determination into each long stride that brought him across the dappled light on the lawn, towards the fragile-looking American.

The house was intriguing, filled, Paige was sure, with secrets and mysteries, a history that she was quite fascinated to learn, but even more intriguing was the man who stepped from the shadows and onto the grass, walking towards her with what could only be described as a brooding countenance. Paige was an actress by training; she'd landed her first advertisement as a toddler, gone on to star in feature films from a young age, and had grown up surrounded by actors and actresses. She was fluent in body language and the meaning of facial expressions, and yet this man was difficult to read. That he was irritated was obvious, but by what? She wasn't late, and she'd barely spoken. What could it be?

Besides irritation, there was something else. A heaviness in his features, a look of stress, fatigue, weariness? But that was completely at odds with the sheer strength of him, the way he walked—as though he were some kind of wild animal in human form, each step like a lightning rod striking the ground so she almost felt a spark travel over the grass and into her own feet.

'Miss Cooper?' His accent was Australian, like an actor she'd once worked with, deep and relaxed, broad vowel sounds more compelling than they should have been.

'Paige,' she said with a nod, clearing her throat and forcing a smile. She was so thirsty. Having spent the last few years of her life in Dubai, she should have known better than to have left her water on the plane, but so it was, and Paige hadn't had a sip of anything for almost two hours. In this heat, that was no mean feat.

'I'm Max Stone.'

This she already knew. Not only was he very well known—the billionaire son, one half of the siblings who'd inherited the Stone family empire a few years ago—his details had been included in the file she'd been given upon accepting this assignment.

'Thanks for coming.' His voice was deep and earthy, like the red dust that straddled the road to this tropical paradise—he sounded anything but grateful. His voice was hyper-masculine, leaving her in little doubt he was a man cast from this land, grown from the earth and tropical weather. His jaw was square, strong like cut granite—somehow, it was nothing less than the voice deserved—with a cleft in the centre of his chin that she imagined, quite unhelpfully, to be the perfect size for a thumbprint. His hair was dark, like a raven's, though there was the faintest hint of silver at the temples, and his eyes were a piercing blue, quite hypnotically fascinating. If they were still in LA, she'd have suspected he wore contact lenses, but that was a vanity she somehow knew to be beyond Max Stone. This man was rough, hewn from the elements: he was not interested in his own appearance.

He was looking at her as though waiting for her to speak, but what else could Paige say? That it was her pleasure? That wasn't strictly true. This job was her bolt-hole. She'd desperately wanted—needed—to drop right off the edge of the earth, so she'd accepted the most remote, out-of-the-way assignment she possibly could. Being buried in the Australian tropics felt a galaxy away from the rest of the world, and particularly from the media storm that was building like a hurricane smack bang on top of her old life.

'Thanks for having me,' she said, eventually, then cursed herself for admitting as much. She didn't want her new employer to know that she was on the run. It was hardly a good recommendation for the job.

But if he thought the sentiment a strange one, he didn't show it. 'Amanda will be home in...' he regarded his wrist-watch, an old-fashioned Rolex '...just under an hour. Come inside, I'll show you around.'

Behind her, Paige was aware of movement, as the man who'd driven her—Reg, he'd introduced himself as—carried her suitcase across the lawn, towards the wide steps that led to the veranda. There were potted plants on the edges of the steps, terracotta with a shrub she didn't recognise but liked instantly for its wildness and the cheery, bright flowers. As they drew closer, she saw the petals were quite waxy, and there were pods attached that looked a little like peas. She couldn't resist reaching out and feeling one. At the merest touch, the pod burst open and, as if it were some kind of party-popper, tiny little seeds flung themselves like confetti, wide into the air.

She stared at it with a small frown then lifted her eyes to Max. He wasn't watching. In fact, he was four paces ahead, about to reach the wide, old-fashioned doors to the home. She dusted off her fingers and hurriedly climbed the last few steps, until she was level with him. He smelled like the ocean, salty and tangy.

When he opened the door into his home, she went to move inside, but Reg, distracted, stepped out, so Paige had to quickly shuttle out of the way, and the only direction she could move, at last minute, was practically on top of Max Stone.

She'd thought of him as a wild animal and now that their bodies connected she *felt* that, deep inside her, a certainty that he vibrated with a rhythm quite outside the ordinary human lexicon. On a deeply subconscious level, her body was aware of his body and the way it buzzed and radiated an energy that was all his own. She quickly stepped away, her breathing rushed, her fingers tingling.

'Sorry, boss. Didn't see ya there.' Reg grinned, tipped his discoloured hat, then moved down the steps, two at a time. He conveyed an air of relaxation despite the spring in his step.

Paige didn't dare look at Max again—she couldn't. Not while she was fighting her body's completely unwelcome response to him. Instead, she sought refuge inside the house.

Compared to outside, the hallway was dark and cool, with wide timber floors and walls. Everything about the house seemed original, though Paige was no expert in architecture, and particularly not Australian architecture. She only knew that she liked this place a great deal.

'The house was originally a hotel,' Max practically grunted, from right behind her, so Paige realised she had just been standing square in the middle of the hallway. 'My grandfather converted it into a house about forty years ago, took out a lot of the walls to make larger rooms. I improved the kitchens, bathrooms, brought the plumbing into the twenty-first century,' he said with something that might have even been an attempt at humour? At least at civility. So she did her best imitation of a smile, moving deeper into the house.

'Downstairs is all living. Lounge room's over there.' He nodded to the left, and Paige ducked her head through the wide entrance way to a very lovely, comfortable space— enormous sofas around a big rug, a wall-mounted television, and shelves lined with books. A large bay window framed a spectacular view over the ocean, which all the rooms on this side of the house would share. She crossed her fingers, hoping her own bedroom would have this same aspect. A board game was set up on the coffee table— Scrabble—but it looked to have been abandoned partway through, perhaps because Amanda had needed to go to bed or get to school.

In the middle of her chest, she felt a familiar emptiness— a sensation she'd grown used to over the last five years, since leaving LA and working as a nanny. She'd been surrounded daily by dozens of little signs of family love and togetherness and she'd never quite been able to stop contrasting that easy affection and parental kindness she observed in her work with her own upbringing—which had been sadly lacking in both.

Max had kept walking so Paige quickened her step once more. 'Study.' He nodded to the right. The door was shut and Paige didn't look in. 'Amanda's room,' he said, indicating the left. With a curious expression, Paige pushed this door inwards—after all, Amanda was her charge and therefore any room of hers was Paige's responsibility. The room had no bed, but was rather a kids' haven. A rocking chair by the window so she could sit and stare out at the stunning vista, another television, and a shelf with every games machine one could imagine, and some books scattered over the floor—titles she recognised because they were beloved by all children the world over, it seemed.

'That's where she likes to spend time.' His voice was *almost* normal, yet there was a slight tightening in the words. Amanda choosing to be in this room bothered him. 'Dining room. We don't eat in there.' He pushed open the door anyway and, out of sheer interest, Paige took a couple of steps inside. This room had a view of the lawn and, beyond it, the rainforest that surrounded this part of the house. Thick, ancient trunks with strange vines wrapping around them and constantly singing birds made Paige sigh. 'It's lovely.'

'We don't like it.' *We.* Paige's heart gave another little clutch. She'd never been part of a 'we'. She likely never would be. How could someone who'd lived through what she had, who'd been betrayed by the two people who were meant to be your staunchest, most loyal defenders, ever trust anyone enough to be a 'we'?

'You don't? What's not to like?' she asked breathily, covering her heartache with an overbright smile.

His eyes narrowed. 'Amanda says it's too stuffy.'

'I suppose it is a little formal,' Paige agreed, moving towards the enormous, dark oak table, running a finger over the heavily polished top. There were no signs in here of family life. No photographs, no books, no scratches on the table to indicate happy, shared meals. There was a fireplace, which she suspected rarely got used, and enormous floor-to-ceiling windows with burgundy drapes, and, against the far wall, two small doors. 'What's over there?'

His lips twisted in something between a grimace and a smile. 'That would be the servants' entrance. For dinner parties.'

'Ah.'

'There's a corridor connecting the dining room to the kitchen,' he continued to explain. 'From when it was a hotel.'

'Clever.'

'Normal, for the time. Come on, we don't have all day.'

She startled a little at his switch of tone, at the sound in his voice of—something she couldn't analyse, but it was clear he wasn't happy.

She stepped back into the corridor, moving quickly because it seemed imperative to be ahead of Max, and then continued onwards. And let out all her breath in one big whoosh, because the kitchen at the back of the house was absolutely stunning. He said he'd upgraded it, but she couldn't have known how perfect it would be. While retaining all the historic charm of the house, it was also new and spacious. Large, open-plan, with a central island bench and windows that ran three sides of the room, so here she had a panoramic view of the ocean as well as glimpses of the ancient, fascinating rainforest. The floorboards were the original timber and the dining table in here was the complete opposite to the shiny, formal table in the other room. This table looked well used. She moved to it on autopilot, resting a hand on the back of one of the two chairs. That there were only two chairs told Paige a lot—they didn't entertain often, and they weren't in the habit of admitting a third to their table.

It conjured images of a loving father and daughter duo, of a pair who would be truly in lockstep. She bit back a sigh, focusing her attention on Max and wondering at the slight speeding up of her heart.

'Please, take a seat.' He gestured to the table. She wondered which seat was his and which was Amanda's. It made sense to choose the chair she was already touching, so she pulled it back, sat down and rested her elbows on the table.

Max moved to the fridge. 'Water?'

'Thank you.' Her parched throat practically leapt for joy.

He withdrew two tall glasses from a cupboard and pressed them against a button in the fridge. Ice-cold water made the fine glass frost immediately. Her throat quivered with anticipation.

He carried the glasses to the table, scowling. There was no other word for his expression. He placed a drink in front of Paige and the moment he released his hand she reached out and gripped the glass, almost finishing it before lifting her gaze to his face to find his eyes resting on her with an expression that made her spine tingle in a not remotely unpleasant way. But it was a warning. She felt it and heeded it: Paige had learned to follow her instincts, especially when they were urging caution.

His hands were planted on his hips, his jaw clenched, his body radiating tension, so Paige leaned forward, and couldn't help asking, 'Mr Stone? What is it?'

His thick, dark brows knitted together and her heart began to beat faster. He was so handsome, but in a very rugged way—nothing like the men she'd grown up around. There was nothing contrived about his beauty. It was quite the opposite, raw and uncultivated and all the more overpowering for that.

'My daughter—' His deep, gruff voice tightened. 'Amanda is—'

Paige listened with patience. The agency had given her a brief background on the little girl: eleven years old, first five years of her life spent in Sydney until her mother's sudden death in a car accident. She was now in grade five at school in a small town called Mamili, in the heart of Wattle Bay. Paige had also been required to sign a watertight confidentiality agreement, which suited her just fine. She had a natural aversion to the spotlight these days and naturally respected anyone else's right to protect their own privacy.

'I've done my best,' he grunted, defensive, as though Amanda had laid some charge of failure at his feet. 'But she's changed. She's…unrecognisable.' He dragged a hand through his hair, his crystal-blue eyes pinning Paige to her seat, so a funny heat began to fill her belly. 'I want you to bring my daughter back to me. The agency said you're the best—is it true?'

CHAPTER TWO

PAIGE KNEW HER references had been glowing, and from prominent, wealthy families with deep connections across the world, of course that carried weight, but modesty had her naturally wanting to demur.

'That's high praise,' she murmured, thinking of all the children she'd cared for. Dozens of little faces filled her mind, and she hardened her heart to the familiar feeling of loss. 'I enjoy my work, Mr Stone, and yes, I believe I'm good at it.' Paige had worked hard to flourish in this career. Mostly, she'd wanted to make a difference to the lives of children, having experienced a childhood that was so far from the norm herself. She would never allow herself to love and yet she poured a sense of love into each and every child she cared for, treating them all as she wished she'd been treated.

Max Stone regarded her with a look that set Paige's nerves on edge. A look of appraisal, as though he was only just seeing her now for the first time. She deliberately held herself very still, not showing a hint of nervousness or awareness or any concern whatsoever. His piercing eyes raked her face until she felt her skin warm and she was desperate to look away, to angle her face towards the rainforest and lose herself in those trunks, but she didn't.

'You don't look old enough,' he said after a long silence had stretched and made the air between them crackle, 'to have enough experience.'

She straightened her spine.

'I'm twenty-four,' she bit out, the words clipped. 'More than old enough to care for a child.'

His expression showed scepticism. 'You're little more than a child yourself.'

'I beg your pardon, but I can't be that much younger than you,' she pointed out, then frowned, because he had an eleven-year-old daughter so that wasn't completely accurate. 'And twenty-four is a long, long way from childhood.'

'My daughter is a handful,' he said with a grimace, and she pitied him then, wondering if there was a sense of disloyalty in the back of his mind, making the words a little halting. 'I need someone who can manage her…emotions.'

Paige's lips twisted into a smile before she could stop them, as she remembered what one of her charges—Carrie—had been like at first. 'I have experience with children and their emotions.'

'That's what I hoped. It's what I need. I—when Amanda's mother died, I thought I could handle this. But as Amanda grows up, I'm starting to wonder if she doesn't need more. If she doesn't need—' He shook his head.

'A woman's perspective,' Paige offered gently, pitying him even more, because she could see how hard it was for someone like Max Stone to face the reality that he wasn't able to single-handedly manage his domestic situation.

'Yes.' He closed his eyes, inhaling sharply so his nostrils flared. 'So let's go over the ground rules.'

Paige snapped out of her pity and felt something else instead. Surprise and then—attraction. Really? In response to what? She *hated* being told what to do. Her independence had been too hard fought to surrender it to anyone and yet his natural sense of control was so intensely powerful and masculine that it couldn't help but speak to a part of her that Paige had long ignored.

She hated being told what to do and yet the tone of Max's voice, his easy authority, didn't feel bossy, so much as... protective. She felt as though he might be the kind of person, and parent, who would have been very good at scaring away all the bogeymen under the bed when Amanda was younger. She wondered if he knew how important that was. How important that safety net was for children, to know that their parents were there, protecting them, making their world a predictable and supportive space.

'Amanda was devastated when her mother died—she cannot come to view you as a replacement for Lauren. You're here for three months, and when you leave, I want it to be no harder for Amanda than farewelling an acquaintance. Quite frankly, I can't pick up the pieces for her a second time.'

Sympathy softened Paige's features. 'I'm a professional, Mr Stone. I have no intention of creating a dependency within your daughter.' She paused a moment, then strengthened her voice. 'However, it's my experience that these situations work best when a genuine bond develops.'

'This is a three-month job,' he said quietly, with a steel underpinning those words, as though his very life depended on this. 'There will be no extension of your contract at the end of the three months. This is our home: Amanda's and mine. We don't need long-term help.'

Surprise showed in her features at the abrupt tone to his voice. 'I understand the terms of my contract,' she murmured, a hint defensively. 'But you must understand when it comes to children—'

He lifted a hand in the air, palm facing Paige.

'This isn't about children, it's about Amanda.'

His love for Amanda was abundantly clear. Something like envy stirred in Paige; she ignored it. 'You asked me here, Mr Stone.'

A rush of electricity, of vitality and life caught her completely off guard. Eventually, he nodded once, his lips compressing with an emotion she couldn't decipher.

'I am simply pointing out that without having met Amanda you can hardly know what is best for her, nor what she needs.'

Paige tried to go gently. 'Do *you* know what she needs?'

That floored him. His eyes, ice blue, bored deep into hers. It was a war of attrition; one Paige had no intention of surrendering.

'No,' he admitted, finally, angrily, but the anger was directed at himself. Paige was torn between pity and irritation.

'Precisely,' she said, standing, because he hadn't sat down and she was beginning to feel the difference in their power dynamic too keenly. 'I was hired—by you—to do a job. Now, I have no intention of getting out there—' she pointed generally towards the ocean '—and telling you how to find big, shiny pearls, but by the same token you shouldn't interfere.'

'She's my *daughter*,' he said darkly.

'And you have asked for help with her. So let me help you.'

'I don't want her to be hurt.'

'You don't want her to feel like you're giving up,' Paige intuited, using the same tone of voice she employed when one of her charges was in need of placating. Calm, reasonable, without emotion. 'She won't.'

He grimaced.

'And I'll be up front with her from the beginning,' she conceded quietly. 'This is a three-month contract. I'm not here to stay. I'm not here to replace her mother. I'm here to help right now, when you need it, and then I'll leave.' She tilted her chin with a hint of defiance. 'And by the same token, Mr Stone, you should be warned: if at the end of the three months you would like me to stay, I won't consider it. I have other obligations beyond this,' she said. Even though that wasn't yet true, she was in demand and knew another booking would eventuate when she wanted it.

And by then, the dust would have settled on the tell-all book, and with any luck she'd be done with licking her wounds, and she wouldn't stay here a moment longer than was necessary. She wouldn't stay anywhere ever again, wouldn't get comfortable, wouldn't let herself relax, because it was just too risky. She had a heart of iron but she wasn't a complete automaton—living with children for any true period of time meant investing her heart and she simply couldn't do that.

'I won't ask you to stay.'

She didn't need to wonder why his rushed agreement made her stomach twist uncomfortably. Being rejected and disposed of with ease was one of Paige's biggest fears in life. With her training as a nanny, she now understood the psychology behind that: she'd never known security as a child. Love had always been conditional for Paige. Conditional on her landing whatever role her parents— managers—had decided was right for her. Conditional on her losing weight to fit the clothes of the brands they'd signed her up to be an ambassador for. Conditional on her agreeing to go on television and do live interviews, even though as a child she was fundamentally ill-equipped for that kind of spotlight.

Paige had never felt loved just as she was, and she probably never would—that sort of conditioning was hard to shake.

And while she wasn't looking for Max Stone—of all people—to 'love' her, she didn't like the ease with which he agreed that she was temporary.

But that was their agreement, plain and simple.

'I work in the study,' he said quietly. 'If I'm not there, I'll be down on the docks.'

'Okay.' She nodded once, ignoring the spark of curiosity ignited in her mind by reference to the docks. The idea of pearl farming had captured her imagination as soon as she'd accepted this assignment. What a strange, unusual and glamorous occupation.

'Amanda's schedule is on the fridge. Reg drives her around, but if you'd prefer—'

Paige bit down on her lip. 'I think it's better for me not to drive her for a while.'

His eyes narrowed and she felt pressured to add, 'I do have a licence. Technically.'

'Technically?'

Now, Paige felt as though she were in the principal's office—not that she'd ever attended a normal school.

'Well, I learned to drive in the States, so there's the whole right-side, left-side thing to contend with. And on top of that, I've been in Dubai for five years. I didn't drive there, either. In the interest of safety—'

'Fine. Reg will continue to drive her.' Then, with a furrowed brow and a concession to civility she hadn't expected, 'And he can take you anywhere throughout the day, if you need anything. There's a town—Mamili—about twenty minutes away, near the school.'

'Are there any tasks I can do, while she's at school? Usually I help out around the house…'

'No.' His flat refusal was another immediate rejection. 'We don't need that. We're fine. Just keep yourself busy…'

'And stay out of your way?' she couldn't help prompting, surprised to find one corner of her lips lifting in a cynical smile.

His eyes narrowed and his Adam's apple shifted as he swallowed. 'My days are busy.'

But he didn't need to explain anything about his life to her. Paige's interaction with parents was usually kept to a minimum. He had offered her the use of a chauffeur, which was a courtesy that wasn't necessary.

'Thank you,' she said quietly, surprised that her voice trembled slightly, but he didn't seem to notice.

'The bedrooms are upstairs,' he said. 'Amanda's and mine at the top of the stairs. You can choose any other room for yourself.'

It was a dismissal and Paige's nerves were frazzled

enough that she was glad for the reprieve. With a small nod of her head, she left Max alone in the stunning kitchen, moving up the beautiful wide staircase as though the devil were at her back.

He was surprisingly grateful when she disappeared quickly, and the moment she left the kitchen he expelled a long, deep sigh. What was it about this woman that unnerved him? Was it simply that she was a nanny, hired to care for his daughter? Of course that was a part of it, but Max wasn't an idiot. There was only one way to explain the surge of adrenalin pounding through his body, the direction his mind kept wandering in, as she spoke and her lips parted breathily and her chest puffed out with indignation, drawing his attention to her gentle curves, to the graceful way she moved, almost like a ballerina. She was attractive and fascinating and he could already tell that it was going to require monumental effort to ignore the way she made him feel.

With a sense that a thundercloud had formed directly above him, he began to walk upstairs, sure he'd given her enough time to have disappeared into a room and keen to grab his pullover for a trip to the farm.

He rounded the corner of the landing and strode to his own room right as Paige stepped out, a guilty flush on her cheeks. 'Oh, Mr Stone!' Her eyes thudded to his. 'I'm sorry. When you said your room and Amanda's were here, I thought you meant those two, I didn't think—'

She waved blithely over her shoulder, in the direction of his bedroom, which she'd evidently just been in.

He realised now how vague his instructions had been; he couldn't really blame her, and yet something like anger fizzed inside him because he didn't want to think of her in his bedroom, while it was just the two of them alone in the house.

'I'm sorry again,' she breathed huskily, so close he could feel her breath, and ancient, long-forgotten, repressed nerves began to fizz and burst beneath his veins. How long had it been since he'd touched a woman?

That was an easy question to answer.

Since Lauren had died.

Since well before Lauren had died, in fact, because their relationship had been messy for some time prior.

Six years? In the back of his mind, he registered the fact with shock, and wondered why it hadn't occurred to him before this.

'I misunderstood,' she responded with a small shake of her head. But the same awareness flooding his veins was apparently making it hard for Paige to focus as well, because her cheeks were flushed and her breathing rushed and, beneath the fine cotton of her shirt, her nipples had hardened to form two perfect shapes, silhouetted by neat, round breasts. He could feel their weight in his palms without touching them, he just knew they'd be satisfying to hold. His jeans strained as the idea of doing exactly that lodged in his brain and refused to go away.

Neither moved.

The air thickened, like at the end of a hot, sultry day when the humidity had reached breaking point and the sauna-like atmosphere meant the sky would need to burst at the seams and flood the earth with rain to stave off spontaneous combustion. But they were inside, there was no rain here, only him, and her, and one of them had to be strong enough to break the spell weaving around them.

'Don't misunderstand again,' he growled, stepping back to let her pass. She startled, looking up at him as though he'd threatened to kill a cat, then quickly moved around him, and down the hallway, spine straight, magnificent auburn hair like flames cascading down her back.

He closed his eyes on a sigh of relief, but when he breathed in to fill his lungs back up, he could taste her in the air. Great. Just great.

Amanda, at eleven, was tracking about three years ahead of what Paige might have expected. She was sullen, moody, had a few spots on her face, and was clearly unimpressed with the idea of a stranger living in her home. Particularly when that stranger's purview was *her*.

'I don't need a babysitter,' Amanda, with eyes as startlingly clear blue as her father's, had snapped, shooting Paige a withering glance. 'I'm old enough to take care of myself.' And with that, she'd slammed the door in Paige's face.

There'd been no chance to form an expectation of how Amanda might behave. Paige had only Max's warning to go off—that she was a handful at the moment. But he hadn't elaborated on what that entailed, nor had he shared any insights into what was making Amanda behave this way. Paige had nothing to go on but her gut feeling, and it told her that something had happened, or was happening, to upset the girl, and she knew it was her job—more than her job, her responsibility—to get to the bottom of it. She owed nothing to Max Stone, but as a woman who'd once been a little girl in distress, who'd been saved by the kindness and interest of a kindly adult, she made it her business to pay that same kindness forward whenever she could.

And it was abundantly clear that Amanda needed kindness.

She also needed patience, something she wondered if Max Stone had any idea how to demonstrate.

But Paige did. She needed answers, and not from Amanda—it was clear that the little girl would need some time to adapt to the new dynamic and Paige knew better than to push it.

Despite the fact having a conversation with Max made her blood do funny things in her veins, she balled her hands into fists and walked back downstairs, along the pleasingly cool corridor, to the room with the closed door. Knocking on it twice, she waited for him to call something out, but when he didn't, she turned the door handle slowly, cautiously, poking her head around the door in time to catch Max evidently lost in thought, standing at the window and staring out.

In those few seconds, her wretched eyes observed details that were none of her business, like how athletic and toned he was, how pleasingly slim his waist was, how his trousers fitted him snugly in all the right places, hugging his bottom and hips, making it impossible not to notice his virility, so she startled, lifting fingers to her lips and blinking away quickly, but not, she suspected, before he caught her in the act of staring at a very personal part of his anatomy. Oh, good heavens. How she wished the earth would open up and swallow her whole.

What was wrong with her?

'What is it now, Paige?'

At least he'd dispensed with the 'Miss Cooper'.

But Paige's mouth had turned to dust, as dry as the desert airstrip she'd flown into, and her tongue was all thick and stagnant in her mouth.

He made a growling noise, then strode towards her, reaching behind Paige and pushing the door closed. 'Let's get one thing straight,' he said, pressing a finger to her chin and lifting her face towards his, so their eyes met and their lips were only inches apart. Her breathing was rushed, her chest moving quickly to allow for the fast pace of her lungs. 'I am not part of what's on offer here. You're here to care for Amanda. If you have any other ideas, then I suggest you forget them.'

Paige was aghast, her lips parting and her eyes flooding with white-hot rage at his disgusting assertion. She wanted to slap the man in front of her for daring to suggest such a disgusting thing, even when the rational part of her brain could see, on some level, why he'd leaped to that conclusion. Finding herself in his bedroom that afternoon had been one thing but, coupled with the way she'd just been ogling him, yes, she could understand how he'd added two and two together and arrived at four. Pride however made her defend herself.

'You are so, so wrong,' she said stonily, when she could trust her voice to emerge without breaking.

'Am I?' His eyes probed hers, a warning in them, but also a surrender, so Paige knew that if she didn't step away from him, something was going to happen. She didn't know what. She couldn't have said, but it felt as if a time bomb were ticking, counting down to an inexorable explosion.

'And so being in my bedroom was really an innocent mistake?'

'Of course it was,' she hissed, wondering why she still wasn't moving away.

He held her chin, and then his other hand lifted, as if drawn by magnetic force, to her hip, his fingers splayed wide.

'You should keep your distance, Paige.'

Her eyes fluttered closed and her senses were filled with him. His smell, his nearness, his strength and warmth. She swallowed, her mouth not working properly. But she thought of Amanda and how much that little girl needed her, needed help, how her behaviour was likely a classic cry for that, and knew she had to push through this.

'I can't do that.'

His nostrils flared. He was so close it was hard to think straight but she forced herself to focus.

'This situation is going to work best if you and I are a team. We have to work together.'

'But we're not talking about work right now.'

No, they hadn't been. They were talking about something distinctly unprofessional, something messy and fraught with difficulties, the kind of complications Paige avoided like the plague. Her personal life was already imploding, she didn't need to throw this kind of dynamite into the mix.

With another deep breath, and a glare for good measure, she stepped quickly away from him, deeper into an office that was clearly a sanctuary for the man. 'Believe me, I'm not interested in that,' she said huskily, waving a hand in the vicinity of the door while her troubled eyes landed on the rainforest.

'That's good, because it's not going to happen.'

Was he trying to convince her? Or himself? After all, he was the one who'd put his hand on her hip, who'd touched her as though he couldn't stop himself. She remembered the way she'd been taken advantage of as a teenager, the unwelcome advances, the pressure to hook up with men just because it was expected of her, or the possibility it could be professionally advantageous. She should have hated being touched. She thought she did, yet there was something about his tanned, broad hand that was so masculine and so—reassuring, even as he was throwing lewd accusations at her. But this wasn't going to work if she allowed this strange energy to take over everything. She had to concentrate.

'We need to discuss Amanda.'

His expression was unreadable, but on his lips she thought she caught a hint of derision and dug her nails into her palms to stop herself from explaining further.

'What would you like to discuss?'

'Her behaviour.'

He stiffened. 'Yes?'

'One of the reasons children lash out like this is that something specific has happened. Something upsetting. A fight with friends, for example. Can you think of anything that's been going on with Amanda?'

His eyes narrowed. 'Nothing out of the ordinary.'

Well, that wasn't saying much. To an eleven-year-old girl, even an ordinary upset could be quite destabilising.

'Has she mentioned *anything*, whether you think it's significant or not?'

'No.' Then, with a deepening frown, 'She hasn't been talking much lately. I've spoken to her teacher. She told me Amanda's generally well liked, though there has been some movement in her social circle. But it's got to be more than that. She's just become so—' He hesitated, and she felt his protective loyalty and something inside her softened. He was a strange beast of a man, with many facets, but she thought she might actually come to like this side of him—the loving, confused father. 'Argumentative,' he added slowly, rubbing a hand over his jaw. 'It's like I'm her least favourite person on earth. I can't say anything right.'

His deep Australian accent drawled over the last few words and Paige's heart ached for him.

'I don't know what's going on, Miss Cooper.' Suddenly, he was in charge again. Confident bordering on arrogant, and slightly disapproving.

Paige nodded once. She believed he was at a loss. He wasn't going to be able to provide any sudden epiphany: if he'd had any useful insights he might not have needed to hire a nanny. And with that in mind, the smart thing to do would be for Paige to leave.

There was certainly no point in staying, in the heart of his office, looking at his furniture, his work desk, the photograph behind it of a jetty with two teenage boys and an older man, and wheelbarrows lined up behind them filled with oysters.

And yet…

'Is that you?' she murmured, moving towards the picture.

He grunted. A confirmation?

With her interest overriding any fear of overstaying her welcome, she moved closer to the picture. 'This one?' She pointed to the young man on the left—she'd have guessed he was about seventeen in the photograph, all long limbs and broad shoulders.

She heard the quietest rustle of clothing as he moved across the room, coming to stand right behind her. 'Yes.' The word was drawn from him reluctantly. He lifted a finger to point to the other boy, his arm brushing hers as he reached past her. Paige caught her breath in her throat. 'And my brother, Luca. My father.' He dropped his hand away, stood there, right behind her, and though she was looking at the photo, she could hear him, feel him, and if she closed her eyes, she could *see* him.

They had to find a way to work together, for Amanda's sake, which meant clearing the air. Turning slowly, with the very best intentions in the world, Paige blinked up at Max. 'I meant what I said before,' she whispered. 'I'm here to help with your daughter, not for—not because—'

His eyes swept closed and when he exhaled, his breath tingled the hair at Paige's temples. She stood her ground quite miraculously, given that her knees felt as though they might give way.

'Good,' he said after a silence that stretched a beat too long. 'Let's make sure we both remember that.'

The way he said it made Paige wonder though: was he finding that hard too?

CHAPTER THREE

BY THE NEXT morning Paige felt as though she'd run a marathon, yet she didn't let anyone see just how drained she was.

Amanda was truly awful.

Or rather, she was behaving in a way that was awful. Sulky, grumpy, temperamental and *mean*. Paige had no benchmark for what the girl had been like before, but from everything Max had said—and the dazed expression on his face—this was coming out of the blue like a freight train off its tracks.

Paige drove into the township of Mamila with Amanda, but purposely didn't make conversation on the trip. She was there to observe. From the back seat of the luxury four-wheel drive, she watched the interactions between Reg and the girl—Reg seemed not to notice any changes in Amanda, and if he did, he wasn't going to let her obvious unwillingness to chat get in the way of the stories he wanted to tell. He deserved a medal for his ability to chatter in the face of such obvious belligerence. He talked about the desert, the trees, where he'd grown up, in a house on the other side of the forest with a hole in the deck you had to jump over to reach the front door.

'Don't know why my old man never got around to fixing it,' he said with an endearing chuckle and shake of his head, before turning off the main road and onto another—equally straight, long and lined with those same remarkable trees. Houses began to appear amongst the trunks, just a few at first and then more and more and then they were on the outskirts of a town, with proper roads and signs, and a couple of overhead lights.

Just a main street, really, with a few shops and cafes on either side. It was historic and charming. Paige couldn't help sighing as they drove past. How she'd have liked to stop and explore! But her first priority was Amanda.

She watched as the girl sat with crossed arms, hunched over, staring out of the window with a scowl every bit as impressive as her father's, eyeing the same little shops Amanda had just been admiring.

They approached the school and Amanda tensed visibly. Paige held her breath, watching with even more care. It was a tiny, telltale reaction, just the stiffening of her shoulders, the tightening of her body, but it confirmed for Paige that school was at least one source of stress for Amanda. Perhaps the only source? If Paige could help Amanda navigate whatever was happening at school, it might help turn her mood around. Could it be so simple?

No, of course not, she chided herself mentally. Nothing was simple with hormonal, prepubescent kids.

'What are you doing?' Amanda demanded fiercely, when Paige stepped out of the car.

Paige kept a neutral expression. 'Walking you in.'

Amanda's jaw dropped. 'Nuh uh. No way. I'm not a baby.' She pulled on her school-bag strap and glanced over her shoulder.

'I know you're not, but my job is to see you through the gate.'

'And you can *see* the gate from here,' Amanda hissed.

Paige counted to five slowly. Amanda was right. She could see the gate, and she knew that schools in Australia didn't require parent or guardian hand-off. Kids were often dropped in a zone and a teacher supervised their entry.

She weighed up her options and decided that placating Amanda was the most important thing for now. 'Okay. I'll stay here.'

'Good.'

'Amanda?'

The girl glared at Paige, defensive and prepared. Paige softened her features into a gentle smile. 'Is there anything in particular you'd like as an after-school snack? A favourite food or drink?'

Amanda's eyes darted to the left, her expression shifted for the briefest moment before it tightened once more into a mask of anger. 'What I *like* after school is *privacy*. Got it?'

Max was just leaving the house when Paige approached it. Dressed in beige shorts and a white polo shirt with aviator sunglasses and a wide-brimmed hat, he was the picture of rugged, outback masculinity. Her feet slowed and her mouth went dry.

'Miss Cooper.' He nodded in her direction, lips compressed in a tight line.

A zing of something ignited in her bloodstream. She ignored it. 'I want to talk to you about Amanda, Max.' She deliberately used his first name, and she couldn't have said why. Only, they were to be living together, and working in some ways as a team when it came to Amanda. It was time to drop the formalities. 'Do you have a minute?'

He hesitated, eyes flicking in her direction, landing on her face first then travelling the length of her body quickly, like the cracking of a whip.

'I'm going to the farm,' was his gruff response. 'If you want to talk, you'll have to come with me.'

Consternation flooded Paige. She was curious to see the farm, and desperate to start working on the problem of Amanda's behaviour, but it would mean being in a car with Max, close to him, being stranded who knew where with him, and each of those considerations lit a strange little fire in Paige's belly.

'I—'

'I don't have all day. Yes or no?'

She shot him a withering look then changed course, moving towards him. 'Fine. I'll come with you.'

He had no idea what had bloody possessed him to issue that invitation. Invitation? Command, more like. He'd backed her into a corner rather than just giving her five minutes to talk—a conversation he actually *wanted* to have because if this woman had any insights on Amanda then he was desperate to hear them. And yet he'd manoeuvred them into this situation, and he couldn't say why.

'Hop in,' he grunted, gesturing to the front passenger seat of his car.

He slid into the driver's seat and started the engine, forcing himself not to focus on Paige Cooper's legs as she climbed into the passenger seat. The morning sun sliced through the tinted windscreen so he noticed for the first time the smattering of freckles across her nose.

Paige turned to face him as she buckled in her seat belt and their eyes met, and the same surge of insanity and desire that had paralysed Max yesterday was back, with a vengeance. He was far too conscious of her physicality. Of her eyes. Her lips. Her ski-jump nose. Her slender, graceful neck. The pulse point in her neck that was undulating visibly. The way the soft fabric of her simple cotton shirt clung to her breasts, the long, silver necklace she wore dangling down low, drawing his attention to the valley of her cleavage. Her sweet fragrance, like vanilla and coconut. His brows drew together, his mind vaguely aware of the strange direction of his thoughts, of the fact he should really be thinking of anything but Paige Cooper, of the fact that, after six years of celibacy, apparently he was like a matchbox flooded with gasoline, just waiting for a single flame to make him explode. And she was the flame.

Paige Cooper, here in his home, and now in the confines of his car, and the intensity between them burned brighter than he'd expected possible.

But it wasn't really her, so much as his natural proclivities. He'd ignored them for too long, prioritising instead all things Amanda. Wanting to be a good dad. A good parent— he had to be *both* parents to her, and he'd been determined not to stuff that up. He would do everything he could to parent differently from his own parents—a father who'd been so intently focused on his business he'd neglected his son and a mother who couldn't bear to see Max after the trauma of her divorce because of how Max reminded her of her husband.

He tore his eyes away from Paige with effort, staring out of the windscreen with a stern expression.

Desiring Paige was inconvenient. Hell, it was about a thousand shades of inconvenient, but it couldn't be helped. He *did* desire her. He was aware of her on every level, and there was no sense pretending it wasn't the case. But no way would he be selfish enough to put his own interests ahead of Amanda's. Paige was here to help his daughter, Paige clearly *wanted* to help Amanda, so Max would just have to control his baser instincts. When this was over and Paige had left, presuming Amanda was back to normal by then, he'd change his lifestyle. Let himself start living again, just a little. A weekend in Sydney from time to time, the freedom to remember that he was a red-blooded male.

Paige was conscious of him every single inch of the drive. Even when the view was quite incomparable, she was only vaguely capable of appreciating it, because the man beside her took up so much damned space. Not just physically, though there was that too. His size was awe-inspiring enough in the outdoors, or in a large room like the kitchen, but here, in a car, he seemed twice as big as a regular man, his long legs speaking of athleticism and confidence, his fingers curved around the gearstick drawing her gaze far too often, so she couldn't help remembering what it had felt like when those same fingers had curved around her hip and held her there, when he'd gripped her chin, tilting her face towards his.

She cracked the window a little, because the air in the car was so full of buzzing electricity, and she needed ventilation to clear her mind. She breathed in, the fragrance of the forest lush and woody. Out of the corner of her eye, she saw Max shift his hand from the gearstick to the steering wheel, gripping it tightly, until his knuckles turned white. The silence stretched and Paige's skin lifted in goosebumps.

She opened her mouth, needing to speak. But Max beat her to it. 'What made you take on this job?'

She was surprised by the question, because it came close to small talk, but perhaps it was more an addendum to a job interview. He was trusting her to care for his daughter; naturally he had questions.

'I've never been here,' she said simplistically, leaving out a fair bit of her reasoning—namely, why she wanted to drop off the face of the world.

'Australia?'

Flashes of memories assaulted her. World premieres in Sydney, Melbourne. Camera flashes. Exhaustion from travelling and being so young. Uncomfortable shoes, late nights, interviews. Her face was pale as she shook her head. 'I've been to Australia.' Her voice emerged a little high-pitched; Paige cleared her throat. 'But never somewhere as remote as this. So tropical.' She lifted her shoulders. 'I wanted to see it.'

'I suppose that's fair.'

'I'm glad you approve,' she observed wryly.

'I don't know if I approve or not. I was simply interested in your decision-making process.'

'Why?'

He turned to face her, lifting one of those thick, dark brows, so her heart fluttered.

'I mean, does it matter? I'm here. Anyway, I think I can help you with Amanda. But it will take time,' she said, switching into work mode, her voice gentling. 'I'm pretty sure I'm right, that it's something at school.'

His hands tightened on the wheel.

'Amanda seemed tense when Reg dropped her off this morning. You said her friendship group is changing; maybe she's feeling excluded and that's upsetting her. She hasn't said anything to you?'

His grip on the steering wheel tightened further. 'No. But I'm starting to think I'm the last person she'd open up to.' His jaw moved as he ground his teeth together. 'But there's only me.'

'That's why you decided to hire a nanny?'

He jerked his head once, in silent agreement. 'I need help and I think Amanda needs…a woman in her life. Some of the stuff she's going through, I've got no idea how to help her. I had a brother, no sisters. My brother's wife is great, but they're busy with their own kids.' He shook his head. 'My mother left when I was twelve. Amanda is literally the female I've spent longest with in the world, so I have no advice or wisdom to give her.'

Paige frowned. 'Where's your mother now?'

Silence stretched between them. 'Hong Kong, last I heard.'

Paige shifted a little in the seat. 'You don't see her much?'

He shook his head.

Paige pleated the fabric of her skirt, not wanting to pry but naturally curious. Fortunately, Max continued without being prompted.

'She decided to live overseas, after the divorce.'

Paige wasn't sure what to say. Her own parents were

pathetic enough, but she was still always surprised to en-counter other examples of maternal or paternal failure. It seemed so outside the natural order of things. 'But why?' she asked, simply.

'Why not?'

'Because you're here. Amanda...'

He glanced at Paige then returned his attention to the road. 'But also my father.'

'It's a big country,' she pointed out.

'And she hates him just that much.'

'But you're her son.'

'I'm also his son.'

Paige sat back in the seat, mulling that over.

'I'm too much his son,' Max admitted grudgingly, after another moment. 'She looks at me and sees him.'

Heaviness shifted inside Paige and she reflected on how impossible it was to really know what was going on inside a person, because her first impression of Max had been one of sheer arrogance and alpha masculinity and now she couldn't help but wonder at the wounds his mother's rejec-tion must have caused him. And because it was the most natural thing in the world to do, because Paige was some-one who gave the sort of comfort she wished she'd received more often when distressed, she reached out and put a hand on his knee, intending it to be a light, reassuring touch, a vote of confidence. But his leg flinched beneath her fin-gers and the breath that hissed from between his teeth was not friendly. It made her aware of him on a level she didn't want to feel and, worse, it made her realise that he was dangerously aware of her too. She pulled her hand away as though she'd been burned.

'Where are we going?' Her voice was stilted, breathy.

'To the farm.'

He'd told her that, but the word was a misnomer. Far from being anything like any kind of farm Paige had ever seen, this 'farm' was actually the beach. A beautiful cove of white sand and turquoise water, palm trees along the coastline, and white boats bobbing on the water's surface, lines of rope on the top, and a hive of activity—people moving in and out of the water, to a shaded jetty in the middle of it all.

'It's so beautiful,' she murmured, instantly wishing she'd brought bathers. But then, the thought of wearing something skimpy in front of Max did funny things to her body so she pushed that thought right out of her mind. When things improved a little, she'd ask Amanda to go to the beach with her. It would be a bonding experience.

'Yes,' he agreed, without looking, cutting the engine and reaching across her to pull a book from the glove box. His hand grazed her knee and now it was Paige's turn to flinch. She felt the electric shock travel all the way through her body.

He expelled a sigh, turning to face her. 'Look, Paige.' His voice was deep and raw. His brows drew together, his eyes boring into hers as if trying to read her thoughts. 'About yesterday—'

She blinked up at him.

'I was wrong to say what I did, how I did.'

His statement was totally unexpected.

'Obviously I'm attracted to you.'

Her lips parted, her mouth forming a circle. This, she had not expected. 'That's—I—'

'And I think it's mutual,' he continued, his lips a grim line.

Her cheeks felt as though they were about to go supa nova.

'I believe in honesty,' he drawled. She squeezed her eyes shut on a wave of unwelcome wants. 'There's no sense ignoring the elephant in the room.'

Paige grimaced, then, finally, nodded. 'Fine, okay. Yes.'

'Good.' His approval sent a thousand little arrows darting through her veins. 'But Amanda is my focus. She has been my focus from the day she was born. Earlier, even. From the moment I found out Lauren was pregnant.'

Something shifted in his voice, and a feeling pressed heavily against Paige's emotional wound, like a finger in a bruise. She blinked away, trying not to think about how much she would have loved her own father to express even an iota of that sentiment for Paige.

'So whatever is going on between us, obviously we have to control it. I'm not going to risk Amanda getting caught in the middle of something, just because we couldn't keep our hands to ourselves.' He looked away, features locked into a mask of self-control. 'Because *I* can't keep *my* hands to myself,' he corrected darkly. 'It's important to me that we both keep it professional.'

She appreciated his honesty, and, in some ways, was glad to have him bring their attraction out into the open, but at the same time, something about his words sat uncomfortably in her gut. 'Of course,' she murmured, because what choice did she have? Besides, he was right. The last thing Paige wanted was any complication, and nor could she afford to jeopardise her job, which she was pretty sure having an affair with her boss would do.

So they were attracted to each other. Big deal. Someone like Max Stone probably had a woman he was attracted to in every city of the world. She'd known men like him.

Bigshot billionaires, the behind-the-scenes financiers who greased the money wheels of Hollywood and made the magic keep happening. She knew what men were like. Just because Max Stone seemed more comfortable in rugged outback clothes and his big, comfortable, charming, old house, didn't mean he wasn't also capable of being just like those men she'd known before, in her other life.

Except none of that really tallied with a man who was insisting on putting his daughter first.

Paige turned away and opened the door in one movement.

'Thanks for the drive,' she called over her shoulder. 'Tell me when you want to leave.'

He needed to inspect the harvest—which was looking exceptional, even by their exacting standards—but every few seconds his eyes strayed to the shore, where Paige was walking in the shallows, kicking the water a little, head bent, eyes trained on the splashing droplets as they flicked into the air then landed back in the frothy shallows, being swallowed up once more by the sea. She left small, wet footprints that he could just make out as the water receded, and the skirt she wore pulled at her legs in the light coastal breeze, so he couldn't help but register how delicate and feminine her shape was... Desire surged through him and he dropped his head forward, acknowledging to himself that resisting his desire for Paige was going to be one of the hardest things he'd ever done.

Paige had always thought the Mediterranean was the most idyllic, stunning beach in the world. It was certainly famed for the juxtaposition of culture, history and natural beauty. But here, in the very north of Australia, Paige wondered if there'd ever been a more breathtakingly lovely sight. The water was so clear she suspected that if she were to wade out up to her neck she'd still be able to see her feet against the white crystal sand. The water made little diamond shapes as it danced and caught the sunlight, reflecting and refracting it into myriad patterns. She desperately wanted to swim, but the most she allowed herself, having looked over her shoulder to be sure Max wasn't nearby, was to tuck her long skirt up a little, into the elastic of her underpants, and go into the water to her knees. It was so delightfully cool, so refreshing, that she actually moaned out loud. She went a little deeper, reaching her fingertips out and drawing them through the water, lifting it and pressing it to her throat and neck, which were too hot courtesy of the beating mid-morning sun.

How was it possible that somewhere could be so pristine and unpopulated? She turned her back on the ocean, looking instead to the coastline, with its glorious green forest almost the whole way to the beach, so wild and untamed. There were some houses she could just make out and, in fact, her eyes chased west. And there it was—Max's tree house. She smiled, because it really was incredibly beautiful, magical seeming, wise and ancient against the backdrop of resplendent nature.

'Paige.' His voice caught her by surprise. It wasn't his fault. She'd been in her own little daydream world. She turned too quickly, guiltily almost, and lost her footing, slipping in her haste, half stumbling into the water, so she was wet all the way to her breasts on one side. Heat flushing her cheeks, embarrassed at her silly, clumsy body, she stood quickly, glaring at him even when it wasn't his fault, stalking out of the ocean without being able to bring herself to meet his eyes.

But then, she thought better of it, turning to face him and changing direction, walking right up to him so they were toe to toe. 'That was an accident,' she said crankily. 'I slipped. It was not some kind of "wet T-shirt" scenario designed to make my clothes stick to my body.'

'Thank you though for drawing my attention to the fact that your clothes are in fact sticking to your body.'

She bit down on her lower lip and looked away.

'Though yes, in fairness, I had already noticed.'

Her cheeks felt as though they were burning.

She crossed her arms over her chest. 'What did you want?'

'When?'

'Then. You called my name.'

'You said to tell you when I'm ready to go.'

'Oh.' She cast one last, longing glance at the beach. 'And are you?'

He hesitated a moment, eyes raking her face, expression impossible to read. And then, 'Yes. We should go.'

Disappointment unfurled in Paige's chest. What had she been hoping? That he'd suggest they go swimming together? He was working, and she wasn't his houseguest. She was an employee in his home, that was all.

'We should,' she agreed, her voice tinged with glumness. But still, neither moved. The air between them crackled and hummed and Paige's lips parted, warmth spreading through her as she imagined what it would feel like to be kissed by him. Out of nowhere, an image of him doing exactly that assailed her and she trembled all over. What on earth was happening to her?

He wanted to kiss her. He wanted to pull her against his body and taste those sweet pink lips, to feel her curves hard against him. He wanted to know the touch of a woman again, to know the heady rush of intimacy, and he wanted that, particularly, with Paige. She'd stirred something to life inside his chest, something he'd been fighting since the moment she'd arrived. He'd blamed her.

He'd accused her of instigating it but that was wrong.

The moment he had seen her he'd felt re-energised, reborn, a red-blooded man again, fully aware of his needs and desires.

He wanted nothing more than to act on them.

But how could he?

He was going around in circles here, knowing he couldn't take advantage of this situation even when every cell in his body was demanding he do *something* about this desire. She felt it too. He might have been out of practice with women but he understood people and the way her eyes lingered on him, stuck to his lips, or his body, when she thought he wasn't looking… She was as much under siege as he was.

So wouldn't he be doing them both a favour if he acted on this?

And then what?

Frustration whipped the base of his spine. Desire unfurled in his belly.

'Don't you need to go?' she whispered, her voice soft, curling around him like the waves of the ocean.

Didn't he?

Shouldn't they?

'Is that what you want?' His voice was made hoarse by desire.

'Max.' Her word was a sigh and then her hand lifted to his chest, almost as if she couldn't help herself. The second she touched him, sparks exploded in his gut. Heaven help him, he was stirring to life—with a vengeance. Every part of him was energised and hyper-charged, hyper-aware of Paige. 'We can't—'

Her voice trailed off and he closed his eyes, trying to latch onto sanity, to his legendary self-control. He did so, but with monumental effort.

'No.' He took her by the wrist and removed her hand, swallowing hard at the simple, possessive contact. 'We can't.' Now his voice was flint, as if the simple act of asserting dominance over his desires had rendered him stone. 'Let's go, Paige. We both have work to do.'

CHAPTER FOUR

THEY ATE TOGETHER that night, the three of them. It was Paige's suggestion, but the moment they sat down Max wished he'd had an acceptable excuse to leave. He'd become used to the awkward, prickly silences when it was just him and Amanda. He'd learned how to zone out to ignore his own deficiencies, and to drown out the proof that his daughter was starting to hate him. But with Paige in the room, he felt every single one of those thoughts banging into him until he wanted to scream. Worse, the air between him and Paige seemed to hum with all the power of an extremely localised electrical storm, so there was no refuge from tension, no respite. He should have avoided this like the plague.

Amanda sat on one side of the table, opposite Paige, with Max at the head.

And for all Paige had orchestrated this happy little scenario, once they were seated, she made very little attempt at conversation, so he found himself wondering almost obsessively about what she was thinking, what she wanted, noticing all the small details, like how she held her fork and shifted her water glass when she was lost in thought.

Max ground his teeth, forcing himself to focus on his

daughter, to ask Amanda the staple round of questions she generally liked to ignore:

How was school?

What did you do at lunch?

Did you learn anything interesting?

What do you have on tomorrow?

Amanda, for her part, had made an artform out of the almost non-existent response.

Good.

Walked around.

Not really.

Nothing.

The whole routine took about forty-seven seconds and then silence returned, except for the scraping of their plates. Once they were finished, Amanda pierced him with her blue eyes then stood. 'May I be excused?' He couldn't tell if it was hostility or something else that was making her voice shake but he nodded curtly.

'Clear the table and then you can go get ready for bed.'

'But I cleared it last night!'

'Amanda.' His voice held a warning, but inside, he felt an unfamiliar emotion—lack of control. The same feeling he'd been grappling with for months as his daughter morphed into a stranger. Worse, transformed into parts of Lauren that Max had thought he'd never see again. It was all made worse by Paige's presence, by how she made Max feel, and by the certainty that he really didn't want her witnessing his abject failure as a parent. 'Now.'

'Fine,' she snapped but with a withering glance at Paige that crossed about ten lines. He glanced at her to see if she'd noticed and of course she had. But unlike his interactions with Paige, which had been defined by emotion, she was now watching with an almost serene expression on her face. Hadn't he thought, when he'd made the decision to hire a nanny, that he needed someone with more patience than he had? Evidently, that was true of Paige.

'Would you like a hand, Amanda?' Paige asked, reasonably.

'No.'

'No, *thank you*,' Max corrected, knowing it wasn't fair or right to be embarrassed by his daughter, even when that was exactly how he felt.

'No, thank you,' she mimicked, rolling her eyes and carrying the plates into the kitchen, dropping them on the bench with enough force to break them—though they didn't.

'Go upstairs,' he ground out, already at breaking point.

'I'm going. Jeez.' Amanda stomped from the room and all the way up the stairs, slamming the door shut behind her.

Max turned to Paige and felt…deflated. Defeated. Emotions he wouldn't have said were in his wheelhouse until recently. But there was something about Paige's expression, even just her *presence*, that offered a hint—just a very small hint—of respite, at least in so much as dealing with Amanda. There were, for the moment, two grown-ups. Two adults. The scales were tipping in his favour, even just by Paige's presence.

He reached for his wine and took a long drink, wished it were something stronger, like a double shot of whisky. Even when he'd been married to Lauren, he'd never felt as though he had another adult in the house. Lauren had been worse than a child, worse than a hormonal adolescent. Her mood swings and unpredictability, always a force to be reckoned with, had grown out of control after Amanda's birth. He'd tried to make her better, encouraged her to get help, halfway dragged her to appointments with the world's best psychologists and psychiatrists, convinced there was a form of postnatal depression at play, but Lauren had refused to give anything a try.

He ground his teeth, turning to Paige, then standing slowly, moving to the kitchen, uncharacteristically lost for words. Ordinarily, he tidied the kitchen after dinner with a sagging sense of relief to have such a boring ritual to lose himself in, but tonight he felt Paige's watchful gaze and the air had taken on the same strange quality it had been exhibiting all day.

'Do you mind if I make an observation?' Her voice was soft and pretty, her accent hard to place. He knew she was American, but perhaps her time in Dubai had softened the edges of it. Learning another language could do that, he'd heard, as if your palate reshaped itself to accommodate a whole new raft of sounds.

'It's what you're here for, isn't it?'

She tilted her head to the side. 'You're different from what I expected.'

It wasn't exactly what he'd thought she'd say. He had been waiting for some indictment of his parenting or some insight into Amanda, and yet the personal observation wasn't unwelcome. 'Am I?'

She gestured to him, standing in the kitchen, sleeves rolled up to the elbows. 'You have way less staff.'

'Staff?'

She made a noise of agreement from low in her throat.

It shouldn't have been sexy but, given Max's gasoline situation, he felt that sound reverberate all the way through his body. 'To cook for you. To clean up after you.'

'I have a housekeeper—Reg's wife.' He shrugged. 'She comes in for a few hours a day, cooks a meal, does some cleaning and laundry.'

She tilted her head to the side, regarding him thoughtfully, then changed the subject abruptly. 'Tell me about Amanda's mother.'

The question hit him right in the solar plexus, coming so soon after Amanda's grumpy departure. He hesitated, midway through stacking a plate into the dishwasher.

'Because you're curious, or because you knowing about Lauren will help you with Amanda?'

She was quiet a moment. 'Both.'

He appreciated her honesty. It was only natural that she would have questions. He'd invited her into his domestic sphere. He'd asked for her help. Now that she was here, he had to work with her. He returned to stacking the plates, one after the other, finding it easier to talk when his hands were occupied.

'Lauren died when Amanda was five.'

Paige nodded sympathetically but Max didn't notice. He was sinking back in time, to those memories, those dark days. 'Our life was different then. We lived in Sydney— that was Lauren's idea.'

'Whereas you wanted to be here?'

He braced his palms on the bench, turned towards the windows. The moon shimmered over the ocean and his heart stilled, as it always did when he soaked in that outlook. 'She liked it there.' He didn't answer the question.

'The shops. The nightlife.' He cleared his throat. 'We had a place on the harbour, and a lot of live-in staff. Two nannies,' he said, careful to keep emotion from his voice. 'Lauren…' But he faltered there.

Even this many years later, even with all the evidence of his wife's failings, loyalty made it hard to face her faults head-on. He sought refuge in frustration and anger, rather than letting his own failings, and the abysmal failure of his marriage, resonate too deeply.

'She died in a car accident. She wasn't driving but the driver was drunk. He lost control coming around a corner—too fast—and rammed into a building. The car burst into flames. Lauren died immediately.' His voice was gruff. Regardless of their differences, of the fact their marriage had most likely been heading towards divorce, he couldn't think of the waste of Lauren's life without a searing sense of shock and sadness. She had grown and birthed his daughter.

When he flicked a glance in Paige's direction, she was expressionless, a mask she was doing her best to keep in place, he guessed, because her eyes had the slightest sheen of tears.

'Amanda was so little.'

Silence fell. Max finished stacking the dishwasher, wiped the bench then dried his hands, coming to stand at the table, lost for words and strangely, despite the heaviness of the conversation, not wanting the night to end just yet.

'And they were close?'

'Lauren was her mother and so she was her world,' he said quietly. 'But in the day-to-day sense, Amanda spent considerably more time with her nannies. And I—' He gripped the back of the chair tightly. 'I was busy with work.' He tried to flatten the defensiveness from his tone. 'I didn't realise at first—'

He shook his head. He wasn't going to discuss his failings. Not with Paige.

As if sensing his reticence, she leaned forward slightly. 'It must have been a very hard time for you.'

She meant Lauren's death. But the truth was, it had all been hard. Their marriage had been a disaster zone, almost from the first.

'You can't do it, bro. I know why you want to, but she's not right for you.'

Luca's warning had been accurate, but Max hadn't had a choice. Lauren had been pregnant with his baby, and there had been no way he was going to fail to meet his responsibilities. He wasn't his father.

'Amanda was devastated,' he said, honestly. 'Lauren was—' He tried to find the right words. 'She was larger than life. Everything she felt, she felt to the nth degree, and she *loved* baby Amanda. She doted on her, spoiled her. Even though she didn't spend that much time with her, the time she did spend left a huge impression on Amanda.'

'And her death a huge absence.'

'It's become worse as Amanda's grown older. She's turned Lauren into some kind of god.' He lifted his shoulders, at a loss. 'She idolises her.'

Paige nodded sympathetically, then stood, the slim curves of her body shown by the soft cotton of her shirt and shorts. 'What are her hobbies?'

Something spasmed in his chest. A feeling of failure. 'Hobbies,' he repeated, as though he hadn't heard.

'Sure. Things she likes to do for fun, outside school. Does she swim? Surf? Read?'

'She reads.' He latched onto the last one, though he couldn't think when he'd last seen her actually finish a book. 'She loves Harry Potter.' But did she? She'd watched the films on repeat the year before, but since then? Flashes of his own childhood, his absent father, rammed into him and Max felt the inexorable pull towards defeat. Maybe you couldn't alter genetic predispositions after all. His father had lacked any kind of parenting gene; Max probably did too.

'Okay.' Paige nodded thoughtfully. 'That's a start.' She hesitated a moment, her lips parted, her eyes round, and he had the now familiar desire to reach out and touch her. To kiss her. To feel those soft lips beneath his. He wanted, more than anything, to kiss her because if he kissed her, maybe he could drown out everything else. Maybe the sheer urgency of their desire would silence the steady drumbeat of the inevitability of his shortcomings as a parent and for a while, a small while, he might even be happy.

'Thank you for dinner,' she said with a smile that had him pausing, because it was somehow familiar. Somehow, and that question jolted him out of his reverie.

'Have we—?' He frowned. It was a stupid question to ask—he knew the answer. And yet... 'Have we met before, Paige?'

Her smile dropped instantly and her eyes darted towards the door. He recognised the emotion: panic. Suspicion took his breath away.

'No, of course not,' she said, the words high-pitched.

Something shifted inside him. A warning. She was lying.

His instincts were rarely wrong and she was a *terrible* liar. He wanted to believe her, he realised, but it was so clear that she was hiding something from him.

This woman he'd invited into his house wasn't being honest with him.

And he was trusting her with his child.

Had he been so blinded by desire that he'd missed obvious, earlier signs of this? Anger, entirely directed at himself, made his face tighten.

'I don't believe you.'

She started, eyes wide. 'Well, I'm telling you the truth.' Her voice faltered. 'We've never met.'

But it all made sense. Why else would he have felt this drugging sense of need for her from the first moment they'd met? He'd seen her and wanted her and it had been so blisteringly overwhelming. Besides, now that he'd seen that look of panic in her eyes, he knew she wasn't being honest with him.

'Damn it, Paige, I need to know the truth. You're caring for my daughter. I have to be able to trust you.'

'You can trust me,' she insisted, and when she flinched a little, he realised he'd come around the table and was now standing only inches away from Paige.

'So you're being completely honest with me? You're not lying?'

Her lips compressed and her hesitation was the beginning and end of the confirmation he needed. 'Why are you so sure I'm lying?' she asked, going on the defensive.

Max's hackles rose. But it wasn't just this conversation, so much as the tumult of feelings he'd been putting up with since Paige arrived in his life. Desire was unwelcome and desperate and so too his sense that he was wading deeper and deeper into the ocean.

'I'm a good judge of people. I can tell you're hiding something.'

'I'm not hiding anything relevant to my job,' she responded, and this time it was Paige who moved closer, her eyes locked to his, her expression defiant and angry, so a thousand questions burst through him.

'Aren't you?' With effort, Max made his voice sound as though he were in control, when his insides were rioting, thrown into total chaos by her nearness.

'You have no right to interrogate me like this.'

'I have every right. You are my employee—'

'Yes, but I am still my own person entitled to my own private life and thoughts.'

'Not if that life involves secrets that somehow endanger my child.'

Paige glared at him, her face pale. 'I would *never* do anything that would put a child in my care at risk. How dare you even suggest it?'

'Because I don't know you,' he hissed. 'You have arrived out of nowhere.'

'I came from an agency. I know you've seen my references.'

'Yes,' he agreed, wishing she didn't smell so good, that he weren't conscious of her warmth and softness and curves. 'But what do they really tell me about you?'

'We are both unknown quantities and I cannot see that it matters. Are you telling me I know all your secrets, Max?'

He flinched. 'That is not the same thing, and you know it.'

'Of course it is,' she disputed quickly, pressing a finger

to his chest. 'You know I'm a good nanny, this isn't about that. You want to know more about me because of this.' She gestured from her chest to his. 'Because of whatever is sparking in the air every time we're together.'

'It's insanity,' he muttered, reaching for her hand, but instead of removing it from his chest he held it there, his eyes issuing a challenge she didn't back down from.

'Yes, but it's the truth.' She jutted her chin at him defiantly and Max couldn't help but take the bait. With her face so close to him, her body so near, his hand wrapped around her wrist, he stared at her mouth and before he knew it, before he could understand what he was doing, his lips pressed to hers and it was as if the ground were splitting in two, so earth-shattering was the sense of relief and desire.

She froze against him, completely still, and then she moaned softly, leaning forward so her body was crushed to his, and he deepened the kiss without thought, angry and frustrated and so hungry for her all at once. It had to stop. He had to stop it, but when she whimpered against his mouth, all thoughts of putting an end to this flew from his mind and, instead, he imagined scooping her up and carrying her to his chest, to his bedroom, or anywhere, and making love to her until she was finally out of his mind.

'We can't...' she muttered as her hands crept to his shirt and pushed it up, so her fingertips glanced across his skin and a surge of need exploded. 'Amanda...'

God, Amanda. Hell. It was like being doused with water. He pulled away from Paige with a stricken expression, staring at her as though she were an alien from outer space.

Paige stared back, her lips parted, her fingers trembling in mid-air before she dropped them to her side and looked away.

With sanity returning, Max began to realise what a monumental mistake that was. Paige worked for him. She was
his staff member. And he *needed* her help, desperately. He
was the one who'd said they couldn't let anything happen,
so why hadn't he been strong enough to fight that?

He dropped his head forward, trying to grab his breath,
and a moment later lifted his face and found her eyes. She
hadn't left the room, which he took as both a good sign
and an indication of her strength of character. She was a
fighter; he was glad.

'I have to be honest with you,' he said after a pause, realising that for all the admission was the last thing he felt like
making, it was important in light of what had just happened.

She crossed her arms over her chest in a clearly defensive gesture but at least she stayed.

'I haven't slept with anyone in a long time. Since my
wife died, in fact. I've been single, and you're here, and
obviously you're a very beautiful woman, but I refuse to
let this go any further when I know it's just because I've
been celibate way too long.' He paused, wondering if this
was coming out okay. He thought it might all be a bit of-
fensive, but it was important to him that Paige understood:
none of this was about her. 'It shouldn't have happened.'
He cleared his throat. 'It won't happen again.'

He stared at the trees, silver in the moonlight, with an anger
radiating from him that came from so deep in his gut it
might as well have been welded to his bones.

He shouldn't have done that.

He shouldn't have kissed her, shouldn't have provoked
her, shouldn't have argued with her when things between

them were so incendiary, it was obviously going to end in only one way.

He should have fought his feelings harder. Pushed her away better. More fully.

But he hadn't, and they'd kissed, and it was as if something had shifted inside Max so now the idea of not kissing Paige again was like acid burning away at him, the inevitability of his desire for her a tsunami overtaking his entire landscape.

He dropped his head forward, cradled it in his hands, tried to grip hold of who he was. Successful. Driven. Focused. A father. A businessman. Relationships had never been front and centre for Max, even before Lauren. He'd married for Amanda, not because he'd wanted a wife, nor a life of love. He'd tried to be a good husband—in his own way—but as their marriage had continued, he'd felt convinced that he was echoing his father every day, even when he tried so hard to be different.

'You are just like him.'

His mother's sneering words ran around and around in his mind, sometimes almost suffocating Max. He stood abruptly, strode to the edge of the veranda and wrapped his hands around the timber.

No matter how hard he fought it, Max kept finding himself in these cul-de-sacs that forced him to face the truth of that statement. He tried not to be like Carrick, his father, and yet wasn't that kiss exactly how he would have behaved?

Not quite.

Carrick would have had no compunction in seducing Paige then and there, regardless of who might have seen or been hurt by his decisions. And how close had Max come to that? If Paige hadn't reminded him of Amanda, would he have stopped what they were doing?

He clenched his teeth, the feeling that the earth was slipping beneath him making his stomach dip uncomfortably.

What he needed was to push Paige out of his mind. And even more than that, a cold shower. He did both, or at least tried, but Paige seemed lodged in the parts of his mind over which he had minimal control, so hours later, in the solitude of his bed, he finally gave up on ignoring her and allowed her total access to his thoughts and dreams, so finally he fell asleep with memories of her body invading his dreams, and finally, for the first time in days, he was truly at peace.

CHAPTER FIVE

PAIGE WAS UNSPEAKABLY glad when, the next morning, she realised Max had already left for the day. With just her and Amanda in the house, she was almost able to pretend last night hadn't happened. Except, when she stood in the kitchen, supervising Amanda's lunch-box preparations, she could *feel* Max in the air, the whisper of his breath against her skin, the sound of his voice, the sensations in her body as he kissed her, as she yearned for more. But there was also the terror that his question had evoked.

He'd recognised her, only he didn't realise it yet. They'd never met, but he'd probably spent hours being bombarded by a younger Paige's face in movies, and advertisements and schmaltzy television shows. In the first decade of this century, Paige had been everywhere, and despite how her face and figure had changed with age, despite the superficial alterations she'd made, it was impossible to escape her features. They were simply a part of her—from her dimples to her smile to her wide-set round eyes.

If Max didn't trust her, it was because he'd glimpsed a figment of the girl she'd once been.

Amanda was particularly surly, but Paige was only operating on one cylinder. She did her best to focus, asking questions, ignoring the monosyllabic answers, making sure Amanda had everything she'd need for the day.

While Amanda had been very clear that she didn't want Paige to go onto the school property, Paige had known she needed to introduce herself and form a personal connection, so she'd emailed both the principal and Amanda's teacher. The responses had been interesting. Both said what a valued and positive member of the class Amanda was, and how well she was doing.

It was something for Paige to focus on, because it showed that Amanda was really just letting out her frustrations at home.

At the school, Amanda exited the car without a backwards glance.

Paige quickly opened her own door, stood there watching the young girl, waiting to see if she'd look back, but she didn't. At the gate, Amanda simply dropped her head lower and kept walking, faster, her body language completely defensive.

Paige sighed to herself then took a seat in the car.

The drive home was filled with Reg's chatter, but Paige only half listened. In the back of her mind, all she could think about was Max, and how stupid she'd been to let him kiss her like that. No, to basically beg him to.

His admission of celibacy had stolen all the air out of Paige's lungs.

Had Max been so heartbroken by his wife's death that he couldn't imagine being with another woman? Something twisted inside Paige. Just imagining that kind of love and devotion made her yearn for something she knew to be impossible.

Love.

Real, life-altering *love*. She blinked rapidly, staring out at the country as it passed, the dark asphalt cutting through thick, ancient trunks.

To feel love like that you had to allow yourself to trust without limits, to be vulnerable and exposed, and Paige knew that was beyond her. Just as she couldn't alter her features beyond recognition, she couldn't change the parts of her personality that her childhood had brought to bear.

For a brief moment though, she found herself wishing, really wishing, that she knew how to let go of her self-protective barriers and be open to something more in life. To really connect with someone without the awful fear of betrayal, of being used, and, worst of all, being hurt.

Back at Max's home, Paige walked into the corridor with her breath held, unconsciously looking to his study; it was empty, and it remained empty all day.

Paige, determined not to seem as though she was waiting for him, busied herself around the house. She tidied Amanda's bedroom, then the room downstairs Amanda used for recreation, then made a batch of blueberry muffins for after-school snacks, before being drawn by the beauty of the day and a restlessness in her soul to step out into the garden. She was halfway through the psychology book on teens and she brought it with her, choosing a sunny seat on the edge of the grass and reading until an alarm on her watch told her it was time to go and collect Amanda.

Right on cue, Reg appeared in his four-wheel drive.

Without taking the time to replace the book in the house, she moved to the car, swung into the front passenger seat and offered a smile to Reg that she hoped concealed the turmoil of her thoughts.

'You're burned,' he said with a nod.

'Oh…' She looked at her arms, which were indeed a little pink. 'So I am.'

'The sun's a shocker out this way. You need to wear sleeves.'

Reg's own skin was leathery, turned that way from a distinct lack of sleeve wearing, she suspected. 'Next time,' she said with a nod.

As they were approaching the school, Paige pointed towards a park at the end of the street. 'Would you mind parking down here? I'm going to wait for Amanda over there.'

Reg pulled into the kerb but gave Paige a dubious look.

'I'm not sure she'll like that. She always makes me stay in the car.'

'I know,' she said, with more confidence than she felt. 'But I'd like to take a quick peek.'

She was more nervous than she conveyed but it was imperative to *see* what was happening at school, to observe Amanda's demeanour as she left. However, she kept Amanda's missive in mind and waited just outside the gate, rather than stepping inside. She wanted to respect the girl's boundaries while also doing her job, and so she stood, and she watched as the crowds filled the school yard and began to filter through the gates and, finally, she saw Amanda.

She emerged from an undercover walkway with her head bent, walking completely alone. Her backpack was slung over one shoulder. A small group of girls walked a little way behind her, not making fun of Amanda in any way, but nor was the group including her. Amanda looked incredibly tiny and very solitary.

Paige had once been a young girl herself, and though, to the rest of the world, it might have seemed that she had everything one could ever want, in fact her life had been a constant merry-go-round of needing to keep up. It didn't matter that she'd had stylists at her fingertips, she'd still never felt quite *good enough*, which was, she knew, the prerogative of almost teenagers the world over. It could be an incredibly demoralising time.

Trying to keep up was futile and silly. Happiness and self-confidence had to come from within. At the same time, though, it quickly became clear to Paige that Amanda was an outlier to these girls, that her shoes were different, her bag was different.

There was nothing wrong with different if that was a personal choice, but, looking at Amanda, Paige wasn't clear on exactly how much of this had been Amanda's choosing and how much was circumstance.

Her brow furrowed. It didn't make sense that she wouldn't, materially, have whatever she wanted. Max Stone's personal wealth was famously extraordinary. Though he kept a low profile, the Stone family owned and operated one of the most prestigious groups of jewellery stores in the world, supplied with their stunning pearls, as well as exquisite diamonds. They were synonymous with wealth and luxury. Beyond that, she remembered reading some article before coming to Australia about their investments in real estate and knew that their portfolio was quite incredible.

So if Amanda wanted different shoes, surely that wouldn't have been an issue?

Paige stood a little straighter, stepped forward, and the shift in movement caused Amanda—as well as a couple of the other girls—to look in her direction. Amanda's face fell immediately and then one of the group moved closer to her, said something under her breath, laughed and returned to her friends.

A pang of worry radiated through Paige.

Amanda stomped towards her. 'What are you doing here?' she hissed, arms crossed, sullen expression more perfect than anything Paige could have pulled off back when she was acting.

'Waiting for you. Isn't that obvious?'

'You should have waited in the car. I don't need you to come in to get me. I'm not a baby.'

'I didn't come in,' Paige pointed out.

Amanda rolled her eyes.

Paige couldn't help saying, 'I've never seen an Australian school. Want to give me a tour?'

Amanda shot her a withering glance. 'No. I want to go home.'

'Okay.' Paige shrugged. 'Can I carry your bag?'

Amanda looked as if her head were going to explode. 'No.'

'No, *thank you*,' Paige reminded her gently, then wished she hadn't, because Amanda's mood was volatile and she switched quickly from angry to hurt, tears sheening her eyes.

'Can we just go? *Please?*' she tacked on with a little

huff, so Paige's arms stung with the desire to reach out and hug the girl close.

She didn't.

Amanda was nowhere near ready for that.

'Sure. Let's go. You can tell me about your day in the car, if you feel like it.'

Amanda didn't.

She sat quietly the whole way home and once they arrived Amanda jumped out of the car, slung her bag over one shoulder and stomped up the stairs and inside.

Paige sighed heavily.

It was only early on in Paige's assignment—and this was clearly going to take time—but she could recognise the other girl's suffering and wanted, more than anything, to be able to help. She saw the hurt in her eyes, she felt her suffering. Having been on the receiving end of a great kindness in her own life, Paige knew she had to work to find a way through to Amanda.

But she couldn't push it.

The evening passed much as the night before had. Amanda sat in silence, except for the few questions Max asked her, and then demanded to be excused. He agreed, once she'd cleared the table, which Amanda did, albeit with pretty bad grace, and then left the room.

Max looked marginally less shell-shocked tonight.

He moved to the kitchen and Paige found it hard not to stare. Memories of last night throbbed all around them. She was awkward and uncomfortable but also glued to the spot. A glutton for punishment?

He was so...masculine, and somehow even the simple act of rolling up his sleeves and tackling the dishes just made him more so. Growing up with all the trappings of the Hollywood life, Paige had never seen her own dad do much more than put a coffee cup in the dishwasher. They had housekeepers and cleaners and a cook, 'to help keep your calories in check'. Even now, memories of her mother's nagging about weight had the power to make Paige's stomach churn.

'Paige.' Max's voice was deep and something in her gut pulled, like an invisible string, drawing her towards him. She dug her fingernails into her palm as she stood, in an effort to control her movements, to be sure she went only to the other side of the counter and not around into the kitchen and right up to him. It didn't matter that she kept a sensible distance though. The air between them still sizzled and sparked.

He seemed to be lost in thought though—having spoken her name, he was simply staring at her face, not speaking—so Paige lifted a brow encouragingly. 'Yes?'

His lips tugged downwards into something like a scowl. 'You got sunburned today.'

Surprise softened her features, and disappointment swirled inside her chest. 'Yes. I was reading outside.'

He nodded, still distracted. 'I've got some lotion. I'll grab it.'

She shook her head as visions of Max lathering her body flooded her brain, making speech almost impossible.

'No, thanks, I'll be fine,' she said, hastily.

'It's just aloe vera.'

She bit into her lip, knowing she should demur, but then found her head nodding once. Their eyes met and something passed between them, a strangely powerful agreement.

His response was a gruff, 'Wait here.'

Paige stared at his retreating back, her eyes clinging to the way his jeans hugged his rear, her heart racing.

He returned a moment later, the bottle held in his hands, his eyes boring into hers. Step by step he crossed the room, until he was right in front of her, and the air crackled. His throat shifted as he swallowed, his Adam's apple jerking visibly beneath his thick black stubble.

'Would you like me to do it?'

Given what had happened between them last night, it was a loaded question.

'I'll be okay.'

His smile was lightly mocking. 'That's not what I was asking.'

Paige's eyes squeezed shut as she sucked in air, air that was tinted with Max's incredibly seductive fragrance, and her stomach somersaulted inside her body. 'I know.' A whisper—surrender.

'Do you *want* my help?'

She groaned, because the same image returned, Max's large, confident hands on her body, and she blinked up into his eyes, sinking into him, losing herself completely to a power far greater than any she'd ever known.

'I thought we agreed last night was a mistake,' she said simply.

His eyes flared. 'It probably was.'

'Probably?'

'I don't know, Paige.' His frustration was obvious. 'It shouldn't have happened, it was stupid, but it was also the best thing I've done in years and if I don't get to touch you again, to kiss you, I think I'll regret it for the rest of my life.' His eyes bored into hers, a silent question in them, and then he spoke it aloud. 'So I'm asking you, do you want my help?'

It was as though her ears were flooded with static electricity. She couldn't think or see straight but there was a beacon in the midst of it all, a truth she had to face, to grab with both hands because, just like Max, she knew she'd regret it if she didn't.

'Yes,' she whispered finally, exulting in the simplicity of that even when it felt, in some ways, as though she'd just made some kind of pact with the devil.

CHAPTER SIX

THEY REMAINED IN SILENCE, the air between them crackling. Finally, Paige nodded, and Max reached down, linking their fingers, staring at them weaved together before tugging her gently from the kitchen, down the hallway and into his office.

The space was a perfect echo of his personality, all dark wood and gleaming surfaces, masculine, strong, impressive. He closed the door and then locked it with an audible click.

Even when her own feelings were swamping the rational part of her brain, Max was switched on enough to remember that he had a daughter in the house, and that she might wander downstairs at any point.

Paige spun, pulling her hand free, but her fingers still tingled as though they were touching his and her tongue felt thick in her mouth.

As Paige watched, Max removed the top off the lotion and poured some into the palm of his hand. He stared at it for several seconds, as though he was fighting an internal battle, a war raging through him between good intentions and bad, and she wished she could say something to reassure him but the truth was Paige didn't know if this was a good idea or not. In fact, she suspected it was a very bad idea, but she still wanted to be in here, with him. And she was aching for him to touch her again.

He was hesitating and she couldn't help wondering, was that because of his late wife? He must have loved her a great deal to have been driven to years of celibacy by her death. Did he consider this to be a betrayal of her memory?

'I can do it myself,' she felt compelled to offer, nodding towards the lotion. 'If you've changed your mind.'

His eyes jerked to hers, and his jaw moved as he grimaced. 'I haven't.'

Relief surged through Paige, complex emotions forming little eddies in the room. It wasn't a time for thought and analysis though, but a time for action. She held out her arm, showing the pinkness on her skin. His gaze dropped to the limb, and then, almost against his will, he moved one hand to her wrist and held it, while with the other he began to apply the lotion, rubbing in broad circular motions. It was almost clinical, but there was nothing cold or detached about her body's response. Her knees wobbled so she swayed forward a little. His hand on her wrist dug in a little tighter but she didn't think he realised—he was holding her as if grabbing on for dear life.

They were both drowning.

She lifted her gaze, staring into his eyes, or rather, at his eyelids, because his attention was focused squarely on her arm, as though if he didn't cover every single millimetre of her skin, some great evil might befall them. Finally, he let go, as though burned, reaching for the lotion and adding some more to his hands, then took hold of her other wrist and began again. But as he reached her elbow and moved higher, his hand grew still.

'I don't want to get it on your shirt.'

She pulled her hand away, biting down on her lip, her heart racing as she lifted her hands into the air, a challenge in her eyes, daring him to follow through on his suggestion.

With a noise that was low and throaty, he took one step closer then put his hands on her waist, swallowing, staring at her, lost, drowning, grabbing the shirt in his fists and lifting it, oh, so slowly up her sides, higher to her arms and, finally, over her head.

He groaned properly then at the sight of her in a skimpy lace and silk bra.

'You're burned here too,' he ground out, pressing a finger to her shoulder and, with one more look into her eyes, he dropped his head and pressed a kiss there, his lips searing her skin.

She trembled.

'Am I?' She bit into her lip. 'Anywhere else?'

He moved behind her, his finger trailing a line across her back, between her shoulders, then his lips followed its path, pressing kiss after kiss to her skin until goosebumps covered her body. 'Here.' Then he kissed her other shoulder, but this time it wasn't a quick, light kiss, but rather a caress, and rather than lifting his lips, he glided them higher, to the pulse point at the base of her neck, which he flicked with his tongue, his warm breath, his mouth, until she was so awash with pleasure it was almost impossible to stand.

'Max.' Her voice emerged as a tortured whisper, for surely this level of desire *was* a torture device?

His body pressed to her side and then he came to her

front, his mouth parting from her body for the briefest moment before he claimed her mouth, kissing her, but not as he had at the water's edge. This was slower, a kiss of exploration, a kiss that spoke of them having all the time in the world to explore this wild, overwhelming connection.

She swayed forward, needing their bodies to be closer, to be touching, and he reached around to unclasp her bra. It might have been years since he'd slept with a woman, but he was still easily able to unfasten the garment, then slide it from her arms, letting it drop to the ground at their feet.

'Turn around,' he invited gruffly.

She did as he said, her nipples taut against the night air. The next moment, his hands were on her back—not in order to apply lotion, but rather as if from a need to touch her inch by inch, massaging her, familiarising himself with her body. His hands came around to the front, to her breasts, cupping them, and he pressed his hard body to her back, his arousal evident at her bottom so she ground backwards on autopilot as his fingers circled then squeezed her nipples until she was riding a wave of pleasure that was hot and explosive.

And Max wasn't done. One hand swirled circles over her flat stomach while the other continued to master her breasts, and his mouth kissed the back of her neck. His fingers slid into the waistband of her shorts, and then her lace thong, connecting with her feminine shape so Paige startled, the touch both unexpected and extremely welcome.

She said his name in shock though, because it had been a long time for Paige as well, and despite the way they'd been kissing and touching, she still hadn't been—couldn't have been—prepared for the overwhelming deluge of feelings.

'It's— I'm—'

He cursed beneath his breath. 'You feel so good.'

She tilted her head back on a rush of sensation as his hand moved lower, his fingers parting her sex and finding her most sensitive cluster of nerves, teasing it, tormenting it, showing his dominant superiority over that part of her too, all the while her breasts tingled from his ministrations and his kisses lit fires in her veins.

'Max,' she groaned, grinding her hips, needing more, needing so much more.

He sucked her earlobe into his mouth, wobbling it between his teeth, then dropped his mouth to her shoulder once more, sucking the skin there as he moved his fingers faster, her moist warmth building until Paige was exploding against his hand, stars filling her eyes. She stood right where she was, feet planted to the floor, as her panting slowed and breathing returned to something more like normal, but Max wasn't slowing down. He turned her in his arms, eyes hooded, almost unrecognisable for how huge his pupils were.

He pulled her by the hand, towards the armchair in the corner, which he sat down into and jerked her on top of him, so she felt his arousal between her legs and cried out because despite the pleasure she'd just experienced she needed *this*, all of this, all of him.

His name was a cry on her lips, a desperate entreaty for relief that she knew he would heed, that they both would. She rocked on her heels, moving her hips, simulating the sex she was desperate to enjoy with him, but there were far too many clothes between them, so she reached down and touched his jeans, undid the button, then the zip, her fingers shaking.

'Wait,' he commanded, finding her mouth and kissing her, his arousal so huge against her sex, his body so powerfully warm. She didn't want to wait though. Impatience was like a river about to burst its banks. He dropped his mouth to her breasts, taking one nipple inside, swirling it with his tongue then pressing his teeth to it just hard enough for Paige to cry out, with the kind of pleasure she'd never known before. It was too much. She was floundering, unsure how to process these feelings.

Sex had never been like this before.

Sex had never been anything other than what was expected of someone like her.

She'd been taken advantage of by older men, made to feel that her livelihood depended on her compliance, on her participation in something that was supposed to be special and meaningful. Oh, it wasn't as though she'd had many lovers, in fact she'd only slept with a couple of men, but she'd made out with more, been touched by even more, as though her body were a commodity that they were entitled to because of the industry in which she'd worked.

This was entirely different.

This was an equal-participation activity, both as maddened by the connection as each other and, even though nothing could come of this, it was meaningful to Paige because this was her decision. She was exercising her agency to enjoy him, to enjoy this. On one level, she knew it was wrong, but in all the ways that mattered most it was a watershed experience, a gift Paige was giving to herself, and no matter what came next, she'd always have had this moment of euphoria.

'I want you,' she said simply, blinking at him wildly as

she pulled her head up, wrenching away from him so he could *see* the need in her face, could hear it in her words, could *feel* it. It felt so good to admit that! For the younger version of herself who'd never known real pleasure like this, she wanted to claim these delights and hold them to her chest. 'Please,' she added, with a wisp of a smile, hoping it hid the raw emotion he'd invoked with his talented ministrations.

He lifted a hand, cupping her cheek, holding her still. 'Paige—' His voice was deep, husky, but there was hesitation in the way he said her name and her heart squeezed, squelched.

'Don't you dare say you can't do this,' she warned, even as that fear began to grip her, turning her lava-like veins to ice.

'Amanda is the most important thing in my life,' he said through gritted teeth.

Paige didn't want to talk about his daughter right now.

'I'm not looking for a relationship.'

She ignored the tugging in the middle of her gut. Wasn't that obvious? He didn't need to spell it out. She wasn't looking for love, either. They were safe. This made sense.

'But this.' He gestured from him to her.

She shook her head, needing him to understand that they were on the same page. 'Is sex.'

'And you're okay with that?'

She nodded.

'You're okay with it only ever being this?'

Something twisted then, something she didn't want to analyse, but she nodded, giving no clue as to the slight wobble of certainty.

'I don't want a relationship either,' she promised. 'And especially not with some Australian guy.' She smiled to show him she was serious. 'I'm only here for three months. My life is over the other side of the world.'

What life? a little voice in the back of her mind demanded urgently, because Paige had been on the run for years, never staying put long enough to make connections, never risking attachment or love.

'Because for the next eight, nine, ten years, however long she needs me, Amanda is the only person I have room for. I'm not going to stuff her up the way— I'm going to do this right.'

She was impressed by his dedication, by his commitment, even when it hurt to hear it—because she'd never known that kind of parental love and sacrifice. 'I get it.'

'So if you think this is going to make you want something else, something more…'

'I don't,' she promised, wishing she could explain to him that she wasn't like other people. Her upbringing had made her physically unable to want or expect love. She would certainly not be looking to Max Stone to provide it. But how could she even begin to explain what she'd been through? Besides, it was a part of her past she didn't welcome to her present. 'Trust me. Everything's going to be okay.'

He probed her eyes a while longer and must have seen something in their depths that convinced him because a moment later he was lifting up and kissing her again, with more urgency, with such desperate, agonising longing that Paige felt herself tipping over the edge already, her nails digging into his shoulders until she was worried she might draw blood. But the way he was making her feel…it was too much.

He broke their kiss only to rip off his shirt and throw it clear across the room, and in that same motion Paige was standing, stripping out of her shorts and underpants, watching as he reached for something from his wallet—a condom—and opened the pack.

'Christ, I have no idea how old this is.'

She reached for it, studied it against the light and grinned. 'Looks fine to me.'

He didn't return her smile. The air pulsed with raging need. She brought the condom to his tip and, with fingers that were still unsteady, pressed it down, trying not to think about how huge he was.

His jeans were still on, but Paige was too impatient to wrestle them from him. Instead, she climbed back onto the seat, straddling Max and hovering just above his arousal, nervous suddenly, even though they'd just discussed this, and they both agreed this was what they wanted.

'You are so lovely.' The statement was said with a note of surprise, as if he hadn't looked at her before now, but his eyes lingered on her face, so she felt his praise deep in her bones, knew it was genuine, and it somehow seemed like the nicest thing anyone had ever said to her—she didn't think he was saying it because he wanted anything from her, he wasn't saying it pro-forma. It had been dredged from within him with utmost sincerity.

'Right back at you,' she murmured, moving closer to his arousal, needing him, already fantasising about the moment she took him in, madness overcoming her.

'Dad?'

She blinked, the voice coming from a long way away, at least the other end of the house, but Max's instincts were faster, more finely honed, so he startled, shifting quickly, somehow displacing Paige without knocking her to the ground. He was standing, chest heaving as he went to control his breathing, face drained of colour before he quickly zipped up his jeans and turned away.

'Dad?'

Still far away, but growing closer.

Paige squeezed her eyes shut, waves of feelings rocking her to the core, from embarrassment to disbelief to impatient shock.

'Just a second, honey.'

His voice was almost completely steady. Almost, but Paige heard the hint of huskiness to it and had to bite her lip to stop from reacting because even that was so sexy.

He grabbed his shirt and pulled it on, stood stock-still for a couple of seconds longer, then, looking completely like himself, strode to the door.

'Wait here,' he barked, eyes sweeping over her on the smallest exhalation, but Paige trembled in response.

'I need you to sign this form.' Amanda's disembodied voice came down the hallway but Paige didn't hear anything else. The door latched closed behind Max, giving Paige complete privacy once more.

Alone in his office, she felt the cobwebs of desire began to clear, leaving her with conflicting feelings. She knew she wouldn't have regretted sleeping with him, but maybe Amanda's interruption had been for the best?

Maybe it was a message sent by some higher power that they should think carefully about what they'd been about to do. Attraction was one thing, but how could they continue living together for the next three months if they slept together?

And would Paige be able to do her job properly?

It was obvious that Amanda needed help, that Max needed help, and Paige was determined to be the person that could render that assistance, but if she was distracted by *this*, whatever the hell 'this' was, then how could she make that work?

She dressed slowly, almost as if she was tempting fate, seeing if it would deliver him back to the office before she could finish putting her clothes on, but it didn't. Not only had Paige pulled on her clothes and finger-combed her hair before he returned, she'd also studied the photos on his wall until they were committed to memory. Mostly, they were photographs of the ocean and pearl-farming operations, beautiful snaps that had a professional quality, the flat-bottomed boats lined up at sunset, workers just silhouettes against the orange-tinged sky, thick-trunked trees that she somehow just knew belonged to the forest at his doorstep, and a picture of two young boys, so similar except for their eyes—one had eyes of ice, the other of coal, but they were both strikingly handsome with square-set jaws and determined mouths.

She lifted a finger to Max, touching his lips, her fingertip tingling, then she quickly dropped her hand from the glass front of the picture as the door clicked and he strode back into the room, those same ice-blue eyes sweeping over Paige in one motion as a muscle jerked in his jaw.

'Okay?' she prompted, skimming his face. Something

tangled in her chest. Pity. A desire for this man, and also a desire to take away his worries, to ease this burden.

'Just time for one last shouting match before bed,' he said with a shake of his head, rubbing his hand over his jaw. They were worker's hands, showing that, while he was a billionaire, he still prided himself on the manual parts of running the pearl farm.

'Paige—' He looked at her, frowned, at a loss for words, evidently, and she didn't want to hear those words anyway. Paige had known the deepest of rejections, had felt it cut right through her soul, but she didn't want to hear it now, from Max.

'Would you like a tea?' she asked quickly, a soft smile showing awkwardness.

He lifted both brows. 'A tea?' he repeated, voice deep, so Paige almost groaned. Did he have any idea how incredibly handsome he was?

'Sure.' She shrugged, hoping she seemed almost like normal, when her heart was still pounding hard against her ribs. 'I always think a good cup of tea can fix anything.'

He laughed then, the reaction surprising her, and him, if his expression was anything to go by. The sound cracked around the room like a whip, sending a little tremble down Paige's spine. It was desire—but not just for him physically. For his laugh. His smile. She pushed the thoughts away: unwelcome and treacherous.

'I hate to break it to you, but that theory seems at odds with reality.'

'We'll see,' she challenged. 'It's always worked for me.'

His eyes narrowed thoughtfully. 'Has it?'

Paige thought about that. There were plenty of times in

her life when it had, in fact, failed, but it had calmed her nerves at their most frazzled and given her time to gain a little more perspective. 'It helps,' she amended ruefully.

'I'll have a coffee,' he said after a beat.

'At this hour?'

'It's a compromise.'

She smiled, relieved in the depths of her stomach that they weren't going to part ways, yet.

'But let's sit outside.' His eyes dropped to her mouth, lingered there, and Paige's heart sped up again. 'I—need some fresh air.'

The balcony that wrapped the perimeter of the house was wide enough to comfortably accommodate furniture and several different pieces had been arranged at intervals around it. There was a white wicker daybed with a perfect view of the beach, and then, a little further around the corner, two deep chairs with beige cushions, a single footrest and a rounded coffee table between them.

She chose the one with the footrest, putting her feet on it and listening to the sound of crashing waves, aware on a subliminal level of how that sound echoed the torrent of her pulse. The mood had changed, but something had been set in motion between them so Paige knew it was no longer a question of 'if' but when they slept together. Anticipation made her nerves skittle even as that certainty was somehow calming.

Max sat beside her, placing their drinks on the coffee table. Paige reached for her tea, cupping her hands around it.

'I wish you could have known what she was like.'

Paige's heart stammered. 'Your wife?'

He stared at her, confusion briefly visible in his symmetrical features, before he shook his head once. 'Amanda. Before...this.'

Paige sipped her tea, hating herself for feeling relieved, but the truth was she didn't want to talk about his late wife, nor to think about the woman. 'I can imagine.'

'She was so sweet. I mean, I don't know the faintest thing about raising kids, despite the books I read after Lauren died, but somehow, Amanda was so great anyway. Just her, I guess. And now...' He lifted his palms up, staring straight ahead. The moon formed a perfect slice of silver across the ocean, rippling as the waves churned. The fact he'd read books did something funny to her emotions. She blinked away quickly.

'She'll get through this.'

'You're sure?'

'Yeah.'

'Why?'

She sipped her tea. 'My first nannying job was in Dubai, and there was a teenage daughter in the house. She was different from Amanda, but the moods, they were similar.'

'Why Dubai?'

She toyed with the fabric of her shirt. 'I liked that it was different from what I was used to.' She wasn't so well known there, and she'd sought refuge in wearing a hijab— she'd craved anonymity, and in Dubai she'd found it. 'My first clients were an American family, so it didn't matter that I didn't speak the language. But slowly, I learned to speak some Arabic, in the time I was with them, so my next job posting was to another family in the same city, and then my next job too, and so on and so on.'

'You stayed there until now?'

She nodded.

'You must have been very young when you took your first job.'

Paige's smile was wistful. 'In fact, I was only nineteen myself.' She tilted her head to the side. 'I felt older.'

'Nineteen seems way too young to be looking after kids.'

'Maybe it gave me an advantage. I really could understand what Carrie—their daughter—was going through. She sort of looked up to me as well,' Paige admitted but with a hint of reluctance because she didn't want to tell him that, in fact, she'd been worshipped by all the children, idolised because her fame was still relatively recent and, as Americans, they'd grown up with her in films. They couldn't believe they had a real-life celebrity as their babysitter. 'So while she would have these awful moods with her parents, she connected with me right away. That helped.'

'And Amanda?'

'It's going to take some time. I guess, losing her mom the way she did, she's probably pretty good at keeping people at a distance.'

'She didn't used to.'

'People change.'

He frowned. 'Without reason?'

'Sometimes, but I'm sure there'll be a reason. Even if it's just growing older and becoming newly conscious of what's missing in her life and feeling the burden of that injustice.'

He was quiet, drinking his coffee, before he placed it on the table between them.

'What made you decide to become a nanny?'

She almost dropped her tea, so moved it to her lap, employing both hands to keep it stable.

'Opportunity,' she said, after a slightly too long pause. 'I was offered the job.'

'You didn't want to go to university?'

'I studied childhood education while I worked, via an online university. The kids I looked after were at school during the day and once I'd organised their activities and tidied their rooms, I still had a lot of time left.'

'And your own parents?' he prompted softly, as though on some level he understood that this was a difficult conversation for Paige. She kept her face averted, staring straight ahead.

'They're not in my life.'

His gaze was heavy on her face, his probing curiosity searing her, and for the first time in for ever Paige felt as though she wanted to answer the question directly.

'For any reason?'

She turned to face him slowly, sensed the chasm between them. How could someone like him understand? She opened her mouth, contemplating how to tell him, to even begin, and then shook her head. 'For about a million,' she said with a grimace that had been quite famous at one point.

He frowned, as though he was still trying to place her, and Paige hurriedly looked away. Her secrets were her own; she wasn't ready to share them. And especially not with Max. It had become important to Paige, more important than she could explain, that he saw her as she really was, not as she'd once been, not as her parents had made her. She wanted to close her eyes and pretend the rest of the world simply didn't exist, that it was just her, and Max, and this stunning tropical paradise…

CHAPTER SEVEN

BUT THE REST of the world did exist and, regardless of how absorbing she found life here with Max and Amanda, she couldn't ignore the fact that time was marching on, and her parents' book was getting closer and closer to being published.

She couldn't face it, which was precisely why she was hiding out here.

Her first instinct on reading about the upcoming 'memoir' had been to dig her head into the sand. And yet there'd been a part of her that had wanted to fight back, too. Her parents had no right to speak about her, to control the narrative of what her life had been like, to speak about her childhood and adolescence. It was yet another example of how they totally disregarded her as a person and saw Paige simply as an extension of themselves.

Even though the book was on the horizon, she felt safe here, as if Max were somehow capable of protecting her, even though he couldn't possibly. He didn't even know who she was, nor what she was up against.

And so she needed to keep hiding, to keep pretending it wasn't happening, otherwise the sadness of all this would swallow her whole. Tuning out the big wide world was an important self-preservation technique so she focused on the here and now with all her might. She would work harder, be better, invest everything into Amanda—and Max—so that the book lost some of its power to hurt her. At least, that was what she hoped.

On the drive to school the next morning, with Amanda sullen and Reg talking non-stop, Paige eventually managed to interrupt his monologue.

'Amanda, we're going to cook dinner tonight. Any requests?'

Her response was predictable. 'I don't want to.'

'It's important to help out around the house,' Paige responded. 'So? What's it to be?'

Amanda sighed as though she'd just been asked to scale a brick wall with her fingernails.

'Don't care.'

'Great. Pickled ox tongue it is.'

Amanda gasped before she could remember not to react, and Reg cackled. 'You might think that's gross, but actually my mother used to make it all the time.'

Paige flicked a conspiratorial smile at the older man. 'Last chance,' she told Amanda. 'Otherwise you'll get whatever I decide.'

'Fine. Whatever. I don't care.'

She hopped out of the car and slammed the door.

Paige sighed heavily. 'Is there a shop somewhere we can stop at?'

'Yes, ma'am.' Reg's face crinkled with amusement as he turned the car in the direction of the only grocery store in town. 'You've got your work cut out for you with that one.'

Paige watched over her shoulder as Amanda crossed the

street to the school gates, shoulders hunched, arms crossed over her slender frame.

'Reg, do you have any idea what's going on with her?'

'Nah.' He shook his head. 'The missus says it's just one of those things. That she'll come good. But it sure is a shame. She used to be one of the sunniest kids, smiled all the time.'

Paige was waiting by the gates when Amanda finished school that afternoon, and she saw the girl emerge from her classroom. As on the day before, she was alone, a group walking just behind her. One of the girls looked up, scanned the waiting parents, presumably for her mother, and looked directly at Paige, then glanced away, before her eyes travelled back again. Paige barely noticed—her attention was focused almost completely on Amanda. She did see, however, when one of the girls ran up to Amanda, grabbed her arm and leaned closer, said something and laughed, then skipped away. Amanda stared after her, face like thunder, then spun around to look at Paige, lips parted, eyes wide.

Self-conscious, Paige glanced down at her clothes, then up at Amanda, who'd resumed her trademark sullen look. But when she came close to Paige, she slowed, stared at her long and hard then crossed her arms.

'Hi.' Paige ignored her sense of misgiving. 'How was school?'

Amanda frowned at her. 'Fine.'

Paige repressed a sigh. 'Ready to help me in the kitchen when we get home?'

'I have homework.'

'Okay, after your homework, then.'

'Fine. Whatever.'

At the car, Amanda slid into the back seat and slammed the door, staring resolutely out of her window and refusing to speak the rest of the way home.

Amanda didn't resurface until Max returned home. She'd been studying in her downstairs living area and Paige had thought it best to give her some space. It was enough that she'd extracted a promise for help in the kitchen.

But with Max's return, Amanda appeared in the hall-way. 'Can you both come in here?'

Paige glanced at Max, her heart speeding up. There was something in Amanda's voice that set her nerves on edge but she maintained an appearance of calm, barely looking in Max's direction. When she did, finally, slide her eyes to his, she saw the same look of confusion in his features. Nonetheless, they walked side by side into Amanda's study.

The girl stood with her hands on her hips, looking from one to the other, then pinpointing Paige with her steely blue gaze.

'Is there something you'd like to tell us, *Paige*?'

Paige's heart skipped a beat. She felt Max stiffen be-side her. Everything was wonky; her breath wouldn't come properly.

'Amanda.' Max's voice held a warning.

'What, Dad? Did you know about this?'

She pressed a button on the remote control and a movie began to play, the scene instantly familiar to Paige. She squeezed her eyes shut, but didn't need to look at the screen to see it playing out in front of her eyes. She remembered everything about this movie. It was one of the last films

Paige had done—a teen feature film, a romance, that had been a smash hit around the world.

She heard Max's reaction—a rough expulsion of breath.

'Turn it off.'

'She's lying to us. She's using us. This is obviously some kind of sick joke, like research or something. Why else would some famous Hollywood actress come and pretend to be a babysitter? Jeez, Dad.'

'That is *enough*.' Max's voice was quiet and controlled but Paige could hear the anger in it.

'Did you know?' Amanda demanded and Paige finally forced herself to be brave and open her eyes, to watch what felt a little like a car wreck. Amanda's face was almost wild and Max's was the opposite, perfectly controlled, but Paige saw beneath that, to the throbbing of his Adam's apple and the way his chest moved faster than normal.

'Amanda, go to your room.'

Amanda stared at her father. 'Are you kidding me? Why? What have I done wrong?'

'Go to your room, *now*.'

It wasn't the right decision. Amanda wasn't at fault— but Paige was trembling from head to toe. She knew then that she should have told Max sooner. It was stupid and ir-responsible to think she could keep this secret, especially with the book coming out.

Amanda glared at both of them and then stormed out of the room. Her footsteps could be heard thumping up the stairs and around the corner. Then, there was the deafening sound of her too-loud music slamming through the house.

Max turned slowly to face Paige.

'This is why I recognised you,' he said, after a long beat of silence.

She closed her eyes and nodded. 'My name, that you'd know me as, was Aria Gray.'

His hands curving around her shoulders had her blinking up at him. She swallowed, because his face wasn't anything but gentle, and that was enough to break her heart.

'Why didn't you tell me?' There was no accusation in his voice though, just curiosity.

'Because I don't want to be her,' she said quietly. 'It was a lifetime ago. I'm not that person any more. I probably never was.' She gestured past him, to the TV. 'That person is a construct of my parents, nothing more. I ran away from all of it a long time ago.'

'Why?'

'Because I hated it,' she whispered. 'They chose that for me. They had me at casting calls from practically the minute I was born. I landed a few commercials, then a TV show, then a movie, and by the time I was Amanda's age I was famous everywhere. I couldn't walk down the street without being chased and followed, and as for normal friendships, a normal life, forget it. I hated acting— I'm actually really shy—but I was the sole breadwinner in our family. They made me understand that I couldn't let them down.'

His hands tightened momentarily on her shoulders in response to that, but he made a visible effort to relax.

'So I acted. And I performed. I travelled the world and had my photo taken and went to premieres and photoshoots and, God, Max, it was so exhausting and I hated it so much. I was so miserable.'

'What did your parents say?'

'That I had to keep going. And I couldn't. I just couldn't. I made the decision to legally emancipate myself when I was sixteen years old.'

It was such a calm way to explain the tumult of that decision. It had been one of the hardest things she'd ever done.

'My parents were furious when I left them. I mean, they had all my money tied up in a trust that I couldn't access.' This time, she couldn't keep the bitterness from her voice. 'I didn't have the heart to fight them for it—I was just so immeasurably, inexplicably glad to be free. But I went off the rails. I mean, I was a mess.' She shook her head. 'I can see now that I had a form of PTSD and was just dealing with it however I could.'

He frowned. 'Where did you live?'

'On friends' sofas,' she whispered. 'Wherever. I drank heavily. Partied too much. Anything that would kind of… numb me…to it all. And of course, the tabloids loved that.' She grimaced. 'They didn't see a girl who was broken beyond repair by her parents' choices, but rather a scandal they could exploit, and I was too stupid to realise it was in my power to change that, to stop giving them a story, to stop acting like such a fool.'

'You were still just a kid,' he growled, surprising her with how protective he sounded. But hadn't that been her first impression of him? Protective, defensive, in a way she'd never known.

She pushed away the warmth she felt in response to that protectiveness. She couldn't let him be her carer—she couldn't come to rely on him.

'In the end, it was an actress friend, who'd been cast as

my mom in an early movie, that came to my rescue and made me see it all had to stop. Anna Cooper. She's the one who got me the job in Dubai, with some friends of hers, and that was the start of my life turning around.'

He stared at her without speaking, and her heart beat faster.

'Anyway, apparently the money's all gone because my parents have written a tell-all book about my childhood and my slide into delinquency,' she said with a grimace. 'It's coming out in a few days.' She bit down on her lip. 'And I know I probably should have told you all this upfront, but the thing is, it's never been an issue in any other job and I came here, I took this job, because I just wanted to...'

'Escape,' he finished the sentence for her, squeezing her arms.

She closed her eyes, nodding. 'I don't want to be that person any more, Max. I never did.' Her lips parted. 'The thought of it all starting up again...' She blinked hard, squeezing her eyes shut.

He didn't say anything; nervousness exploded. Paige whispered, 'If you want me to go, I will. I mean, I want to stay. I want to help Amanda, but if this is all too much, if you're worried that something is going to spill over into your life...'

'I'm not worried,' he said with so much strength and confidence it stopped her tears in their tracks. 'I'm angry with her, if I'm honest. She had no business exposing you like that.'

Paige shook her head. 'It's not her fault. I think some-one said something at school. One of her friends. I'm sure she recognised me.'

'Even so, she should have spoken to you, or privately to me. This is what I'm talking about—I don't know who she is any more. Six months ago I would have said my daughter doesn't have an unkind bone in her body.'

Paige shook her head. 'She didn't mean anything by it. She's obviously confused.' She pressed her fingers to her temples. 'This is my fault. I should have been honest. It was naïve to think no one would recognise me. I'm so sorry. If this changes things, if you want me to leave, I will. No hard feelings.'

He swore gently. 'Listen to me.'

She scanned his eyes, waiting.

'Everyone deserves to make their own life. Of course I'm not going to fire you because your parents were selfish assholes.'

She dropped her head forward, sucking in a shaking breath, but he moved then, catching her face, holding it between his hands, lifting it towards his.

'Don't cry.' It was a command, but it was also a plea, and her heart stammered because she felt so much in that simple instruction. She felt, most of all, that he didn't *want* her to cry with every single part of himself.

She sobbed anyway and he kissed her, the kind of kiss that was drugging and overwhelming, that made her whole body shake—or maybe that was the emotion of the day, the intense, all-consuming gamut of feelings she'd run since waking up that morning. No, since the night before in his office, when they'd almost made love.

Max stood, then reached down and lifted Paige as though she weighed nothing, carrying her against his chest down the hallway, until they reached the door to his study and he shouldered it inwards. It felt like the easiest, most right thing in the world.

CHAPTER EIGHT

BEFORE LAUREN HE'D been a red-blooded male, a man in his early twenties with the world at his feet and the confidence that he could have pretty much whomever he wanted. He just had to snap his fingers and they were his.

He'd made love to women out of passion, desire, lust, always with the idea of sex being fun, not serious, never serious. Lauren had been one of those women. Meaningless and unimportant until she'd told him she was pregnant and he'd had a shockingly clarifying moment. He knew what their father's rejection had done to Luca's mother, and how Luca had never forgiven their father for his years of neglect. Max wasn't going to let any child of his be born into the world thinking they weren't fiercely loved and protected, even when that had meant marrying a woman he wasn't sure he cared for at all. But he'd shelved those worries, because he and Lauren were going to be parents and nothing mattered more than doing the right thing by the tiny life-form they'd created.

Lauren and he hadn't really had much of a sex life.

While he'd found her attractive enough at first, the more he'd got to know her and the superficial values she held in life, the less he'd wanted her. But he'd consoled himself with the fact they could both still be good parents—she had adored Amanda—and he'd buried himself harder and harder into his work.

He'd once made love to women out of passion and need, but never like this. Never out of a complete jumble of emotions that was almost impossible to make sense of. There was lust, of course, and desire, the sort of white-hot passion that could melt a man's bones, but there was also a wish to comfort and soothe, to promise Paige with his body that everything would be okay, even when he didn't know for sure it would be. It was a gift he wanted her to have, a moment of pleasure and relief before her world cracked apart again, as surely it would when the book was released.

He kissed her until she was breathless and he undressed her as though she were some kind of precious artefact: gently, reverently, his hands running over her soft, still-sunburned skin so she pulled back from him, pressed a hand hard to his chest and said, 'You're not going to break me.'

Their eyes met and held and for no reason he could think of, he said, 'I'm not going to break you.' Maybe it was because she had been broken, he thought, and she deserved to know that he had no intention of being someone else in her life who hurt her.

Her skin was so soft and smooth. He worshipped her body, kissing her all over, tasting her, wishing they had days and days to explore each other, not only hours, as he parted her legs with his knee and moved his body over hers. 'You're sure?'

She bit down into her lip and nodded, eyes flashing with his, daring him to change his mind so he understood the same desperation he felt was pummelling her from the inside out.

'God, yes, I'm sure,' she groaned, tilting her back and lifting her hips in a desperate, hungry invitation for him.

He didn't need to be told twice.

Moving quickly, he sheathed his length then hitched himself at the entrance to her sex, eyes holding hers, watching her as he sank into her slowly, her muscles squeezing around his length so he swore into the room between clenched teeth because she felt so inexplicably good, so damned tight and wet that he had to hold himself up on his arms and focus or he was half worried he'd lose it already.

'I haven't done this in a long time,' he reminded her grimly, cursing that he hadn't foreseen this and taken matters into his own hands this morning to relieve some of the pressure that had been building inside him since Paige Cooper had first walked into his life.

'So you've said,' she murmured, rocking her hips then latching her ankles behind his back, pulling him all the way in so he swore, dropped down, his heavy, hard body on top of her small, soft one, his voice a caress against her ear as he spoke words that were probably unintelligible— he had no concept of what he was saying, only that a spell was building around them and with each movement of his body, each answering shift of hers, the world was taking on a whole new shape. He pulsed with sensation, with the need to release, but there was determination too, a need for her to find her own release before he gave into his. With the willpower he was famed for, Max held on, watching Paige, feeling her body's responses, her convulsing, her tightening around his length and her muscles' responses as she fell apart in his arms, crying his name over and over in a way that was more beautiful than anything he'd ever heard.

He cursed inwardly, thanking every star in the heavens that he'd managed to hold on, moving once she'd quietened down, moving until her muted cries grew faster again and this time, when she exploded, he was right there with her, breath fast, chest moving rapidly, body shaking with the force of his release, of his pleasure, of his unmitigated euphoria.

Paige had needed to shower and have a quiet cup of tea before she felt as though she could face Amanda, but she knew then that she couldn't put it off any longer. The music was still blaring so Paige gave only a cursory knock—which wouldn't have been audible anyway—before opening the door.

Amanda was lying on the bed, staring at the ceiling, and, while she was no longer crying, her little face was tear-stained and blotchy.

At Paige's entrance, she turned her head, bit down on her lip but didn't look away.

'Hi.' Paige lifted a hand in the air.

Amanda sat up before grudgingly reaching for an iPad and pressing pause on the playlist.

'I suppose you have some questions,' Paige prompted gently, coming to sit on the edge of the bed, but far enough away from Amanda not to seem as though she was trying too hard.

Amanda shook her head.

'Are you sure? Because if I was you, I'd be curious. I'd want to know why someone who'd been really famous once upon a time chose to be someone else now, why they chose to keep that secret.'

Silence.

And then, 'Why did you?'

'Well, the thing is, that whole movie-star thing really wasn't what it was cracked up to be. In fact, I hated it. So as soon as I was old enough, I quit and started a new life.'

'But you use a different name. It's like you're lying about who you are all the time.'

'It's complicated, Amanda. I didn't choose to be famous. That was a decision my parents made for me. When I was old enough to choose, I realised I wanted to just be a normal person, and that meant having a new name and not talking about my old life. I changed my name legally, so it's not really a lie.'

'But you came here and you expected us to live with you and open up to you—'

Paige was impressed by the girl's maturity. 'You feel betrayed,' she said gently.

Amanda's eyes flew to Paige's. She saw confirmation in their depths.

'Believe it or not, one of the things I love most about my job is that I get to focus on other people. I'd rather think about you than me.'

'I'm boring.'

'Not to me.'

Amanda rolled her eyes. 'Come on. I Googled you. You were, like, really, really famous.'

'Yes, I was. And do you know what that meant? I spent most of my life feeling incredibly solitary. I didn't have any real friends. I wasn't close to my parents. I was completely alone and miserable. So now, what I care about most is working with kids who maybe need a friend, who might be going through a difficult time a bit like I did.'

'I'm *not* famous,' she said, which wasn't entirely true. While Max had done a great job of keeping Amanda out of the public eye, the Stone family were tabloid fodder when major life events took place.

'But you are struggling with your friends, right?'

Amanda's face became stony, and she looked away. Paige didn't want to push it.

'I'm here if you want to talk, any time, Amanda.'

She stood up, moved towards the door. 'Are you still okay to help me with dinner?'

When she looked over her shoulder, Amanda's little face had crumpled. 'Do you actually want me to?'

Paige's heart felt as if it might break for the poor, vulnerable girl. 'Yep, for sure.' She kept her voice light.

Amanda nodded. Then, as Paige slipped from the room, Amanda called out, 'Paige? I'm sorry for…that. I thought they were laughing at me, because I didn't know, and they'd all recognised you yesterday. I felt stupid, and I was mad. I should have just asked you.'

Paige hovered in the doorframe. 'Probably, but you were upset, as you said. Besides, I'm the one who's sorry. Even though it doesn't really impact my job, I still should have explained. You were right before: I want you to open up to me. I'd like us to be friends. And that's a two-way street. So from now on, let's have a rule: we'll be honest with each other, and ask each other anything. Okay?'

Amanda's relief was palpable. So too was Paige's. 'I'll see you downstairs in, say, a half-hour?'

Amanda nodded. 'Thanks, Paige.'

It was the most normal conversation she'd had with her young charge and Paige couldn't help grinning as she left the room. It felt as though she'd had a breakthrough with Max, and a breakthrough with Amanda, and her worst fears had happened—they knew the truth of who she was—and the world hadn't ended.

Paige had lost count of the number of times she'd made this dinner. When she'd first moved to Dubai and been charged with three kids under fourteen, she'd needed to find a way to entertain them that they all enjoyed. Cooking had been it. However, as Paige had had next to no cooking experience, she'd had to rely on a 'beginner's cookbook' she'd bought online. This had been one of the recipes, and a firm favourite for the kids.

It was easy enough.

Marinate the chicken while the rice cooked, then start preparing the vegetables and chicken. The whole dinner took less than thirty minutes to cook.

Usually.

But now, she was distracted.

How could she not be?

Max wasn't in the room, but that was even worse, because she couldn't get what they'd done out of her head. He hadn't been awkward about it—anything but. He'd been kind. Gentle. But he'd left his study almost immediately after they'd finished, saying he needed to check something at the farm, and that had been the end of it. He'd seemed distant. Distracted.

She sighed softly.

Could she blame him?

He hadn't had sex since his wife's death. There had to be a heap of emotional baggage to go along with what they'd just done. So he was taking time to process it. Regretting it? Wishing he hadn't done it? She hated the thought of that.

'What now?' Amanda asked, clearly doing her best to be helpful.

'Now…' Paige smiled encouragingly '…we check the rice.'

'The timer went off already.'

'Yep, once the timer buzzes and we turn off the heat, the rice needs to sit a few minutes. Now, we fluff it with a fork.'

Amanda let out a tiny giggle—it was music to Paige's ears. 'Fluff it?'

'Sure. Here. Give it a try.' She handed a piece of cutlery to the girl, then stepped back, waiting for her to approach the pan.

'Um, how do I "fluff" rice?'

'Exactly like it sounds,' Paige explained. 'Take off the lid, and lightly move the rice around until it's separated. Just watch for the steam as you remove the lid.'

Amanda did as Paige had instructed, flicking a glance at Paige. 'Like this?'

'Perfect. You're a natural.'

Amanda rolled her eyes but her demeanour was sweet. 'Like making rice is hard.'

'Perhaps not, but fluffing it well is an artform,' Paige teased. 'Okay, time to cook the chicken.'

They worked mostly in silence after that, but Amanda's face was the most relaxed Paige had seen since arriving. In fact, she even looked, to Paige's attentive eyes, as though she was enjoying herself. In the back of her mind, Paige began to collate some other recipes they could try, easy things that someone Amanda's age would enjoy making—and eating—and for the first time since arriving in Australia, Paige allowed herself to relax, just a little. She felt that she'd won a crucial battle with Amanda tonight, and turned a corner with Max, too.

The book was coming out soon, yes, and anxiety about that hovered on the edges of her mind all the time, but there was something about this house and family that made the rest of the world, and all her worries, feel so very far away.

He didn't know what he'd expected when he came home but it wasn't this. Max had needed space, to process what had happened firstly with Amanda and then with Paige, but he'd come home knowing he'd need to roll up his sleeves and deal with his daughter and her behaviour.

Only instead of finding the house in sullen silence, he saw Paige and Amanda were in the kitchen cooking, side by side, and while they weren't talking non-stop, they were making companionable remarks to each other. Amanda was even smiling.

He stood unobserved with a shoulder against the wall, silently watching, his heart twisting painfully in his chest. Because it had been so long since he'd seen Amanda at ease? No. That wasn't it.

It was seeing them together. It was the first time Max had witnessed Amanda and Paige and the bottom was falling out of his world because they looked so good and right together, it was like walking into one of those houses of mirrors at an amusement park—a thousand different images flooded his brain, including a future filled with moments like this.

What if he got Paige to stay?

What if she wasn't here for just three months, but for ever? What if he could give Amanda a proper family?

His stomach churned because he thought he'd been enough, that by prioritising Amanda the way he had, by moving out here away from the trappings of his former life, by keeping her home with him rather than sending her to boarding school, he'd provided her with all that she could need. He hadn't realised that a gap had been forming in their lives, that the two of them were rattling around like pinballs in this big, empty house. Until now.

And just like one of those haunted houses, the visions shattered and tore away from him with psychedelic speed.

He couldn't ask Paige to stay longer. Even if they hadn't slept together, it would have been too complicated, but, given what had happened between them this afternoon, their relationship had to remain strictly business from now on.

And if he needed any further reminder of why that mattered so much, seeing his daughter and Paige locked in a scene of such happy domesticity reminded him squarely of why those boundaries mattered.

He'd told Paige when she arrived that this was temporary, and that he didn't want Amanda getting hurt. Well, fine, but if he let Paige become a part of the family for the next few months then wasn't hurt inevitable?

His glance flicked to the horizon, as if seeking signs of the storm he felt brewing, but it was clear, all the way to the edge of the ocean.

He frowned, turning his attention back to the kitchen right as Paige glanced up and their eyes met so the air sparked between them and he had to shove a hand in his pocket to anchor himself to reality and his realisation that he needed to make sure nothing more happened between them.

'Hi,' she half whispered, then cleared her throat and blinked quickly, as if to return her voice to normal. But he'd heard the husky sweetness in her tone and it was doing strange, looping things to his insides.

He turned his attention to Amanda. This was all about her, after all. He had to stop thinking about Paige, even when that seemed almost impossible. 'It smells so good in here, honey. Did you cook dinner?'

Amanda's eyes showed wariness, as though she was expecting him to reprimand her for what had happened earlier. And Max would talk to her about it, but not now. 'Yeah. Well, mainly it was Paige, but I helped.'

'You were great,' Paige said. 'Remember, the rice?'

A flicker of a smile teased Amanda's lips and Paige's eyes flew to Max's to see if he'd noticed. Of course he had. He hadn't seen his daughter smile properly for months.

'What are we having?' Now it was his own voice that was gruffer than usual, tinged by the tightening emotion in his gut.

'Umm, Paige?'

'You know what we're having,' Paige encouraged, busying herself with filling water glasses.

'Oh. Um…these chicken-wing things, and veggies, but they actually smell quite good because Paige cooks them in butter and garlic.' She moved across to the rice with a little flourish of her hands. 'And fancy rice.'

'Fancy rice, huh?'

'Well, not really.' Another flicker of a smile. 'But just… rice I did something fancy to.'

'I see. Well.' Max patted his flat stomach but stopped when he saw Paige's eyes drop to the gesture and his body reacted instantly, remembering how she'd dragged her tongue down his wall of abdominals, tasting his skin, and his gut squeezed involuntarily. 'I'm starving.' His eyes clashed with Paige's and the air exploded with electrical energy.

'Great.' Her voice wobbled. 'Let's eat.' Her cheeks were a little pink as she dished out their food and placed the meals on the counter. She was obviously avoiding him, taking care not to look at Max, not to stand too close to him. It was as though they were two magnetic poles but with the same charge. If he moved one way, she went the other. Maybe she'd come to the same conclusion he had? That Amanda had to take precedence.

Over dinner, he expanded his repertoire of questions, buoyed by the glimmer of happiness Amanda had shown, but also to fill the crackling silence. Paige also interjected, asking questions that were generic, impersonal, about the history of the house, the property, the farm, but they were both speaking to Amanda, as if encouraging her to open up, and to Max's surprise, it was working.

But while Amanda and Paige seemed relaxed and at ease, for Max, every minute that passed, the opposite could be said. He felt his own nerves stretching to breaking point. The more peaceful things seemed on the surface, the stormier his insides became. He couldn't help imagining what it would be like if this was normal for them, if Paige, or maybe even some other woman, was permanently a part of their lives. If Lauren hadn't died. Except Lauren would never have made things feel like this. Lauren was too volatile and selfish, and family dinners were definitely not her forte.

And another woman?

He didn't really want to think about that right now.

No, when he imagined this dinner being replicated again and again, it was Paige who populated his thoughts. Damn it.

Beneath the table, his fingers tightened around his knee.

'You should show Paige the attic,' Amanda said, mouth full of rice. Max resisted the temptation to remind her to wait to speak until she was finished eating.

The attic. Something exploded inside him—a wave of desire so strong it took his breath away and terrified him at the same time. Yes, terrified him. Max Stone, who would have said a week ago he wasn't afraid of anything. But the idea of being alone with Paige again when all these feelings were frothing inside him making it hard to know what was real and right any more, he needed space, not time *alone* with her in the dark confines of the old attic. When he spoke, his voice was sharp with irritation. 'I'm sure Paige doesn't want to see it.'

Paige's eyes flew to his, hurt obvious in their depths. Great. He kept his face impassive, reached for his water and took a sip.

'Another time, perhaps.' Paige's response was aimed at

Amanda, her smile slightly wobbly but given for the benefit of Max's daughter.

'Oh, but it's super-cool.' Amanda seemed to have temporarily forgotten her sullen nature altogether but Max wasn't even capable of glorying in that right now. 'It actually used to be servants' rooms, so it's big, runs the whole way across the house, and there are skylights so you get the best view of the stars up there. I used to love playing in it when I was a kid.'

That was interesting. Since when had Amanda stopped thinking of herself as a kid?

Paige was looking squarely at Amanda. 'But you don't now?'

'Nah.' She glanced away, focusing on the wall across from her.

'Well, maybe *you* could show me on the weekend?' And despite himself and his fierce rejection of Amanda's suggestion that he take Paige to the attic, something like annoyance slammed into Max. He'd shut down the idea but at Paige's easy acceptance, he wanted to fight for this. He wanted to take her up there even when he knew he couldn't because of what might happen.

This was a damned mess. He'd been right earlier: he needed space to sort his own head out before he could deal with Paige again.

Amanda shrugged, not willing to commit to the plan. 'I don't really like to go up there any more.'

'I see.' He felt Paige's gaze slide to his, but he determinedly kept his gaze focused across the room.

'Dad?'

'Yes?' He could no longer avoid the conversation. He looked right at Amanda.

'It's okay, Amanda.' Paige offered the young girl a smile.

'You'll show Paige the attic, won't you?'

Finally, he looked at Paige, because he had no choice, and something in his soul ignited. Her lips parted, his gaze dropped briefly and he felt as though he were losing a part of himself. He was terrified by how much he wanted her and how much he'd been thinking of her, he was, if he was honest, terrified of what he'd felt when they'd made love. He'd been trying to rationalise it away as overwhelming because of his celibacy but with one single glance something rolled in his chest that made a mockery of all those very sensible explanations.

He was falling from a great height; disaster was unavoidable.

'Dad?' Amanda's voice was sharp.

The ground was rushing up at him; crashing was inevitable. 'Yes.' The word was louder than he'd meant. He cleared his throat, shrugged as if he weren't making some kind of a deal with the devil. 'If Paige wants to see it, sure.'

'You don't have to do this,' Paige muttered as they ascended the final, narrow staircase towards the now infamous attic.

'It's fine. Let's just get it over with.'

What had she been expecting? Roses? An invitation on a date? What was wrong with her? Paige was usually the one avoiding commitment like the plague. Why was she upset by the way he was distancing himself from her when she didn't even want more from him?

Paige blinked quickly, hating that her emotions were

so close to the surface, hating the tears that threatened to spill over. But everything had felt so good before dinner. She'd been reflecting on how great it was to have achieved so much with Amanda, to have had such a breakthrough, and as for Max… Her heart stitched painfully. What they'd shared had been…life changing. Not because she expected more from him, but because in that moment, when she'd been feeling lower than low, when her past had rushed up to her and threatened to swallow her whole, he'd found the perfect way to draw her to the present and to remind her of who she was, and it had been a beautiful gift she'd wanted to cherish for ever.

She'd expected him to have some issues with it, because of his late wife, but she hadn't been prepared for him to show up at dinner and treat her like some kind of pariah.

'After you,' he said at the top of the stairs, pushing an old timber door inward. It creaked a little, the noise spooky. It was not well lit—a single light bulb dangled from a long white cord in the middle of the room. Paige hesitated a moment before crossing the threshold, her arm brushing Max's as she went, so she was grateful it was too dim for him to see the goosebumps that lifted over her skin.

She could see why Amanda had insisted she come up here. She was distracted enough by the beauty of the space to remark, 'Oh, wow. It's amazing.'

She stepped deeper into the room and it felt as though she were slipping back through time. Despite the fact the house hadn't operated as a hotel for decades, several single beds, wrought iron with brass knobs, were lined up along the wall, reminding Paige of an old-fashioned orphanage. The room though was huge—Amanda had been right, it clearly spanned the whole house, but there were no internal walls. All the furniture was old-fashioned: a leather arm-chair, a big, wide desk, a wardrobe with a mirror—this one put Paige in mind of *The Chronicles of Narnia*. It was like something out of a dream.

'I can feel them,' she said, lifting her fingers to her lips.

'Who?' Max was close, just a step behind her. She turned quickly, blinked, then it was Paige who took a step away, because the temptation to reach out and touch him was too great and she was worried she wouldn't be able to control herself—and he clearly didn't want anything to do with her, despite what they'd shared only hours earlier.

'Them,' she said unevenly, clearing her throat. 'The peo-ple who used to live here.'

His smile pulled pinpricks at her heart because it was so unexpected. 'A hundred or so years ago?'

'Sure, why not?' She moved deeper into the room, glad for the reprieve of space, running a finger over a dusty beam. 'I wonder what their lives were like.'

'Stinking hot, I'd imagine.'

She shot him an arch look. 'Can't you play along, just for a moment?'

'I see a heap of old junk that should have been got rid of years ago.'

That offended every cell in Paige's body. 'You can't be serious?'

'It's just furniture.'

'No, it's so much more.' She shook her head. 'It's the physical manifestation of times gone by. It's beds that were slept in by people with dreams and hopes, who'd lie here at night and look through the skylights and say their prayers for whatever wishes were in their hearts. It's lives lived and woven into the fabric of time. It's history, Max,' she said, breathlessly. 'Can't you feel—?'

'No.' The single word was harsher than it needed to be, hissed between his teeth, and Paige realised belatedly that in her desire to convince him of this magic, she'd moved towards him, close enough to reach out and touch, again. That hadn't been her intention. She'd just wanted him to see…

'It's just furniture,' he said again, as if to push the conversation firmly to the side. Pragmatic and unfeeling. Except he wasn't either of those things. On the surface, perhaps, but Paige had glimpsed more, she'd seen deeper.

'Max—' She didn't know what she'd been going to say and never found out because at that moment the light bulb dangling in the middle of the room went out, plunging them into complete darkness, and the ghosts of those people were suddenly all around them. 'Oh, my God,' she gasped, moving unconsciously closer to Max, needing to feel him for a different reason now.

She heard his rough exhalation, and the strong, muscled arm that clamped around her back was supposed to be reassuring but it made her body tingle as awareness jolted through her.

The stars were incredible from in here. Large, old skylights, circular in shape, showed the heavens as a blanket of lights—not enough to illuminate the room but striking for their vividness; every single one of Paige's senses was on high alert.

'What happened?' She gasped, clinging to his shirtfront as if for dear life.

'The bulb blew. It's old. No one ever comes up here.'

'It's dark.' Such an inane comment, but awareness of Max had tipped her over so she was barely conscious of anything but him. How could she think clearly enough to formulate a rational statement?

'Yes.' His voice had changed. The gruffness had given way to something else. Something throaty and deep, his breath audible. 'You're safe.'

From ghosts? The bogeyman? Maybe. But whatever was swirling between them had Paige on edge. Max wasn't safe; what she wanted from him wasn't, either. It was all complicated and scary. 'Am I?'

Silence fell, and in the absence of noise Paige heard her own body's escalating rhythms, the rapid thundering of her pulse, the frantic storming of her heart, her lungs, pushing air out faster than they could draw it in, the air seeming to squeal inside her ears.

His hand at her back was vice-like; maybe he was afraid too?

Max? Afraid? She dismissed the thought instantly. He was always in control. Even that afternoon, when they'd made love, his body, having been deprived for so long of a woman's touch, had still been able to contain itself, despite his warnings.

There was no way he would fear the darkness of the attic.

Something else though, maybe?

His breath was warm on her temple; the only hint she had that he'd moved closer, that he was looking down at her.

'What happened this afternoon,' he said quietly, and his fingers stroked her back, moving higher up her spine, then lower, until Paige was trembling all over.

'Don't say it was a mistake,' she murmured, because she couldn't bear to hear that.

'No.' The word was wrenched from him, the concession one he struggled to give. 'Not a mistake.'

Her heart fluttered.

'But it can't happen again.'

His hand lifted her shirt a bit, so his fingers grazed her bare skin.

'It can't.' More forcefully, the words almost choked by his throat.

'Are you telling me, or yourself?' she whispered, tilting her face up, body pressed to his by the way he was touching her, moving her forwards.

His voice was a groan. 'Primarily me, apparently.'

'Tell me why.'

'You know the answer. We both do. It's…complicated. There's Amanda. My life—it doesn't include room for you.'

She blinked, shocked by how much that hurt when she'd met this man only days ago, when he'd already been clear about this.

'For anyone,' he clarified. 'I've been married once; I hated it.'

Curiosity sparked inside Paige—she had presumed his marriage to have been happy—but other emotions were taking more of her runtime. She felt the need to point out how far ahead of himself he was getting. 'Do you think I want to marry you because we had sex?'

She heard his rough laugh, just a short, sharp sound. Maybe it wasn't a laugh? Maybe it was surprise that she'd spoken so directly? But really, was there any point in not calling a spade a spade?

'It's easy to get carried away. To think sex might lead to something more. Not necessarily marriage, but a relationship. Seeing you in the kitchen with Amanda...'

Ah. Something about that made sense. Even she'd felt the niceness of that, the similarity to being a normal family. But for Paige, that was part of the job. Everywhere she went, she slipped into the routines and occupied a space that made her family-adjacent. She was used to it, but for Max it must have been confronting. It had just been the two of them for a long time—was he worried about where the lines would be? How to make sure Paige didn't forget herself? Yes, that had to be it!

Taking a deep breath, and steeling herself to be calm, she explained carefully, 'We have a relationship now. You're my boss. I work for you.'

'That's different.'

'It doesn't have to be.' She didn't know what she was saying, only she could see a clear path through this, a thread of logic she could grab hold of, and then everything would be okay. 'We're both on the same page. You don't want a relationship...all your energy is reserved for Amanda. Well, I don't want a relationship either. I mean, not a serious relationship. I like...spending time with you.'

And she really did, she realised. In the midst of the mess that was her personal life, something about Max had become a talisman, a beacon of calm—safety seemed to radiate from his core goodness. 'I've liked getting to know you. But I—' She dug deep into her heart, remembering her awful past, and something about his proximity and just *who* he was gave her courage and comfort. 'I don't think I'll ever be able to get seriously involved with anyone.'

'Oh?' It was a quiet noise of encouragement into the dark.

'Are you kidding? I legally divorced my mom and dad. I had to face the fact at sixteen years of age that my own parents saw me as an income stream and nothing else.' She shook her head angrily. 'The guys I dated after that, they weren't much better. I was their way to get exposure, maybe some introductions to Hollywood heavyweights, it was never about me.' She sucked in a breath, furrowing her brow as she tried to get to the bottom of what she was feeling, what she needed to tell him. 'And now my parents are selling me out, yet again. I'm just a commodity, not a person, not their child, they don't love me.'

'Paige—'

'No,' she interrupted whatever he'd been about to say. 'It's okay. It took a long time to just accept the bald truth of that fact. They don't love me. And if my own parents don't love me, why would anyone else?'

'Stop.' He groaned, catching her face in his hands, holding her steady. 'Don't say that.'

'Why not? I'm happier alone; truly, I am. I can enjoy getting to know you, sleeping with you, without it changing how I *feel* and what I want in life.'

'Which is to be alone for ever?'

'Sure, why not? Is that any different from you?'

'I have Amanda.'

'And I have the kids I look after.'

'You've just told me that your relationships are all skin-deep.'

She tilted her chin, frustrated that he was criticising her approach to life. What was wrong with it? 'So?'

It was too dark to see his face, and he was silent, so she didn't know what he was thinking, and she hated that.

'What about the woman who helped you? The actress?'

Paige thought of Anna Cooper, her features not shifting. 'I'm very grateful to her.'

'But you don't love her.'

'She's a very kind woman—'

He sighed, the breath fanning her forehead. Paige felt as though he was going to keep arguing this point and she really didn't want to discuss her life's philosophy vis-à-vis relationships. 'I understand that most people don't live like I do. I even understand that for most people, their goal in life seems to be to meet their perfect mate and give all of themselves to that one other person, that their happiness is derived from those connections. But that will never be me. Whenever I think of getting close to someone, really close, I mean relying on them and making them a big part of my life, I feel as though I'm suffocating.'

Even now, she felt the pinpricks of panic lighting her eyelids. 'It's just who I am.' She held onto that, a beacon she needed. Being solitary was her choice, it was her power. 'So if you're worried that sleeping together is going to make me, I don't know, fall madly, head-over-heels in love with you then you can forget it. I'm just not wired that way. I can keep my work with Amanda completely separate from…this.'

Somehow, in the midst of all the madness and confusion, she'd found the magic key to unlock the door to what she desperately wanted. 'Max, being with you makes me feel good. Something between us just…works. We don't need to overthink this. We both know it's temporary but that doesn't mean it's not also incredibly beautiful and...'

'Right,' he said on a groan of surrender, and then, holding her face as though she were the most precious thing in the world, he dropped his head and kissed her, and despite everything Paige had just said, it was her heart that rejoiced the loudest, leaping through her body like a firework, exploding so she couldn't help but be aware of the way it was practically abusing her ribcage.

But Paige wasn't worried. She knew her heart wasn't ever really going to be a problem. She'd locked it up nice and tight years ago and that was one key she had no intention of rediscovering.

CHAPTER NINE

WHEN PAIGE RETURNED from dropping Amanda at school the following morning, Max was waiting for her, and as she stepped from the car her stomach gave a lurch, then dropped all the way down to her toes.

He was so incredibly beautiful, she wanted to remember him like this for ever. But that was a thought Paige pushed aside abruptly.

When she left this place, she'd put Max out of her mind. She'd move on. Never get attached—it was her guiding missive. Leave before she could be asked to leave.

'Got any plans for the day?'

Paige shook her head slowly and a warm breeze lifted from the beach and carried her hair against her cheek so she brushed it away.

'Now you do.' He strode down the steps. 'Come with me.'

Her heart, her untouchable heart, raced.

'Where?'

He closed the distance between them. 'You'll see.'

'A surprise?'

His eyes were as vibrant as the ocean beyond the house, his nod was just a shift of his head.

Evidently, their conversation last night had convinced him that there was no risk of Paige falling for him, because he'd let go of any inhibitions and she liked that, because she'd been honest with him. She enjoyed spending time together. She found him exhilarating. Yes, that was the perfect word. He was unlike anyone she'd ever known. Intelligent, charismatic, charming, handsome but also good, his moral fibre impressive and admirable. Just the way he loved Amanda and made her his top priority showed Paige what a great guy he was—and also the polar opposite to her own father.

'I like surprises,' she said, then qualified it with a wrinkling of her nose. 'Some surprises.' The memoir that was about to hit shelves was a surprise she could have lived without.

'Great. Let's go.'

Paige had known Australia was a vast and beautiful place but she couldn't have conceptualised quite how expansive and stunning until she was in the air in a helicopter being piloted by Max, hovering high above this land of stunning nature and stark contrasts. The ocean was mesmerising for its colour changes and vastness. Near the coastline, it was turquoise, almost transparent, so she could see a pod of dolphins in the warm, shallow waters of the oyster farm. Paige held her breath as he brought them in low enough to observe the details on their gunmetal-grey bodies, emerging from the water then diving down again. She couldn't help smiling.

Max piloted them further out over the ocean and the colour change was dramatic—here it was a dark, earthy blue, no less beautiful, but somehow menacing. The white caps of the waves frothed towards the shore as Paige watched. Back over the land, she delighted in the lush green rainforest, the sound of the birds imprinted on her mind now so, even up here, she could remember those sounds as if they were in her ears again now.

But the rainforest and dramatic cliffs and waterfalls were all near the ocean. After another ten or so minutes, they were back over the desert, bright red, strikingly beautiful from this height, particularly when contrasted with the azure blue of the sky. Even better, the helicopter had ice-cold air conditioning so, while Paige could see the heat hazing off the ground, she couldn't feel it as she had that first day, when she'd felt as though her skin were going to sear from her body.

'Incredible,' she murmured, to herself, but, courtesy of the headphones they wore, Max heard and turned to her, grinning.

'Every tourist should fly over the country like this.'

She liked that he considered her a tourist. It was yet another reminder of how temporary her time here was.

'Hungry?'

Paige was surprised to realise it was lunch time. She had no concept of how far they were from home. 'Yeah. I'll need to get back for Amanda—'

He nodded. 'Plenty of time.'

With expert control, Max brought the helicopter lower, and through the swirls of dust Paige could just make out a collection of a few buildings, small and rickety, made of timber and tin.

'Where are we?'

'This used to be the old town,' he said, landing them on the ground to the left of a two-storey building with a rickety-looking veranda. 'The drought closed most of the farms around here down. The town is limping along, but there aren't many people out this way any more.'

'What's this place?'

'The pub.'

'How can such a small town have a pub?'

'It's important to the remaining locals.'

'Sure, but it's hard to see how it could cover its costs. Isn't that why most of these places get shut down?'

He nodded once. 'It's important to keep places like this though. Not just for the locals,' he conceded, 'but because it's a part of the history of the area. This pub used to do a roaring trade, then the highway moved, and it was all but forgotten.'

'It's charming,' she said, glancing up at him as a thought occurred to her and she just *knew* her gut feeling was right. 'Max, do you *own* the pub?'

He looked at her for several beats, shrugged his shoulders, then turned to the building. 'It's part of the place's history. Come have a look.'

The pub was cool and dark and just stepping inside she knew her suspicions were correct, because while the fit-out retained the charm of the pub's history, it was also immaculate and clearly no expense had been spared.

The ceiling was ornate pressed metal, the floor was wide, dark timber boards, and the artwork on the wall comprised stunning landscapes of the outback—originals that she guessed hadn't come cheap. Max led Paige to a table near the back—there were only two other patrons, both sitting at the bar. No sooner had they sat down than the waitress appeared brandishing a couple of menus, with an extensive selection of food—further evidence that the kitchen was bankrolled by someone who didn't rely on the place turning a profit.

'What's good?' Paige asked with a small smile.

'Everything.'

She heard the pride in his voice and her insides leaped. 'That's high praise for a country pub.'

'Trust me.'

And because everything between them felt just a little *too* right, because they were a little too in sync, she wanted to remind him that she didn't *trust* anyone, but it was enough just to remind herself.

She turned her attention to the menu, selecting a garlic prawn dish. When the waitress arrived, Max ordered a bottle of white wine, and his own meal, a rather more substantial-sounding 'surf and turf'.

The waitress was friendly with Max, in a way that Paige couldn't pretend she didn't notice, and couldn't pretend she didn't *feel* a hint of envy about. But that was normal. On a purely primal level, they were lovers, and, just like in the animal kingdom, she temporarily felt she'd staked some kind of claim to him. It didn't mean anything beyond that—she just didn't want another woman making eyes at Max while they were having lunch.

But given that he'd been celibate for the past six years, she probably didn't need to imagine him suddenly leaping over the bar and making love to the other woman. If that was going to happen, he'd have the decency to wait until Paige left, she was pretty sure.

Having been intimate with Max, she found it hard to imagine him living without sex. He was so passionate, so powerful, so…skilled…in that department. To have denied himself that pleasure was bad enough, but to have denied other women seemed almost criminal. That same little blade of envy pressed into Paige as she thought of his wife and wondered about their marriage. He must have loved the other woman a great deal. Except…hadn't he said he'd hated being married?

Curiosity burst through her, irrepressible and urgent. 'What was your wife like?' Paige asked, before she could think better of it.

If Max was surprised, he didn't show it. He lifted his gaze to Paige's face, let his eyes linger there a moment, his lips tugging downward as he lost himself in his thoughts. 'Volatile.'

It was the last thing she'd expected him to say.

'Very beautiful,' he amended, his voice softening, so that jealousy dug in a little deeper.

'How did you meet?'

He tugged a hand through his hair. 'We were part of the same social circle. She was friends with my friends. I don't actually remember the first time we met, I just became aware of knowing her one day.'

'Not love at first sight, then?'

The waitress appeared with an ice-cold bottle of Riesling and two glasses. Max poured the wine, and Paige sipped it just because she wanted something to do with her hands.

'You and I have our cynicism in common. I don't believe in love at first sight any more than you do.'

'Why do you think I'm cynical?' she prompted.

He lifted his brows. 'Our conversation last night?'

'Knowing that I don't believe in love for myself personally is different from saying I don't believe in it for other people. I think love is out there, and that some people, maybe even lots of people, get struck by that mythical lightning strike. Just not me.'

'You're a little young to speak in such absolutes.'

She shook her head. 'I'm an expert on this one subject: myself. I know who I am and what I want from life. It's not that.'

'Lightning doesn't always listen to what we want,' he pointed out, rocking the base of his wine glass against the polished tabletop, eyes locked to hers so she had the strangest feeling he was picking her apart and studying her, piece by piece, even the parts Paige didn't fully understand about herself.

'So what was it like?' she asked. 'I presume you loved her very much.'

'Why do you say that?'

'Because you were married.' Paige floundered a little, realising that one thing didn't necessarily equate to the other. 'And because you haven't—you've been—'

He almost looked to be enjoying her discomfort because he leaned closer across the table, and their legs brushed so Paige shifted a bit, her insides quivering with recognition at the contact.

'Celibate?' he prompted in a stage whisper, so Paige

quickly looked around and ascertained they were out of earshot.

'Yes.'

'I'm not embarrassed by that, Paige. It's not for lack of opportunity.'

Heat flooded her cheeks. 'Okay, Mr Ego. No need to go into what a desirable bachelor you are.'

His eyes crinkled at the corners with a suppressed smile. 'I only mean that I have made a choice and I have no issues with it.'

'And this? You and me?'

'Lightning,' he responded, then leaned closer, beneath the table his palm grazed her knee and goosebumps danced across her skin. 'Of a purely sexual kind.'

Her heart fluttered, her stomach tightened, but in the back of her mind there was something else, something sharp and a little uncomfortable.

'I suppose it was the same with Lauren,' he said, frowning, and that uncomfortable feeling grew bigger. 'She was very beautiful and quite...intriguing at first. She was—fun. Always the centre of the party, laughing, dancing, carefree, quite free-spirited. I suppose I wanted her,' he said, sipping his wine, lost in reflection. 'Because everyone else did.' His frown deepened. 'Back then, I always had to win at everything.' The final statement was muttered, an indictment against himself. 'It's how I was raised.'

'I guess a lot of people in your position have that mindset. Most of the successful directors and financiers I got to know were similarly driven.'

He was quiet, considering that.

'So you wanted Lauren and...?'

'And we got together. It was a short relationship. We dated for a couple of months, but a lot of that was spent with me travelling. We weren't exclusive.'

Paige leaned closer, fascinated.

'Do you know anything about my brother?'

'I know you have one,' Paige said with a lift of her shoulders.

'He's a few months younger than me. Our father had an affair with his mother—she was a cleaner at his hotel in Rome.'

Paige blinked.

'He claims he didn't know about Luca, that she never told him, so until Luca was twelve, we never met. Then his mother passed away, and in the will instructions were left that he was to be sent to my father, with a copy of his birth certificate. After the requisite genetic testing, Luca came to live with us. My mother left the same week.'

It was all said so matter-of-factly, but Paige's heart, which in fact had not been rendered completely offline, gave a thud of pity. 'How absolutely awful, for everyone.' Beneath the table, she laced her fingers through Max's. 'You must have resented him at first.'

'Naturally. I went from being an only child to losing my mother and suddenly having a brother, a brother who was almost the same age and who was of great interest to my father. He pitted us against one another and my anger over what his arrival had done to my family meant I was, initially, more than willing to fight Luca. To try to beat him at everything, all the time.'

'To need to win,' she repeated gently.

He nodded, fingers tracing the bottom of his wine glass

distractedly. The waitress appeared with garlic bread and some olives, placing the little platter between them on the tabletop and disappearing again. Another couple of people came through the door; Paige turned to look at them, blinking. She'd almost forgotten where they were.

'Eventually, we stopped competing. We became friends and finally, brothers. We were a team, too, united against our dad.'

'What was he like?'

Max's hand tightened momentarily on the stem of the wine glass then released, but with visible effort. 'An acquired taste.'

Paige's smile was a flash on her face. 'Oh?'

'I spent my teenage years hating him—with Luca. But as I got older and things got a little more complicated, I saw how nuanced life can be. I hate so many of the things he did, the decisions he made, the way he was with Luc and me, but at the same time, nobody's perfect. I didn't want to spend the rest of my life hating him.'

'So you forgave him?'

'It's not quite so clear-cut. I just…came to enjoy the parts of our relationship that worked. He was good at what he did professionally. I respected him for how he grew the business, and for how he let me step into his role when he realised I could do it better.'

Paige dipped her head to hide a smile at that. It was an honest admission that from anyone else might have smacked of arrogance but from Max was just accurate.

'But the thing with Luc, that's complicated. He found it a lot harder to move on with Dad.'

'Why, do you think?'

'He saw his mother suffer. She raised him alone, money was tight, she was shunned by her very traditional family, had to move to Sicily to get any kind of support. And then he was thrust into the lap of luxury and made to think of himself not as a Cavallaro but as a Stone. He was bitter about it for a long time.'

'And now?'

'They reconciled, shortly before Dad died. It brought the old man a lot of peace.'

Someone at the bar laughed loudly and it pierced the solemn air that had surrounded them.

Paige sat a little straighter, took a drink of her wine, then reached for an olive. It was plump and juicy, and she savoured the flavour, until she became aware of the way Max was staring at her lips. His hand on her thigh moved higher and, unconsciously, she shifted further forward in her seat, bringing them closer together.

'So…' he picked up his train of thought anew '…when Lauren told me she was pregnant with my baby, I wasn't going to let her raise Amanda without me. Marriage made sense to me. I wanted to be in my child's life all the time, not just sometimes.'

Paige had almost completely forgotten what had started his conversation. 'And did she want to get married?'

'Yes. She didn't hesitate.'

Paige frowned. 'Did you know—?' But she stopped herself in time, realising how insensitive the question she'd been about to ask might appear.

'I didn't know Amanda was mine for sure,' Max said quietly. 'Not until she was born and she opened her eyes, so like my own, and I felt this instant, powerful connection. I loved her. I knew I'd made the right decision. She was mine, and while Lauren and I weren't in love, we were going to raise her together. Lauren loved her too. She was a good mother. Better than my own, at least,' he said with a gruff laugh. 'Better than yours, too, by the sound of it.'

Paige stroked the back of his hand without responding. She didn't need to.

'I didn't do any testing. I didn't need to.'

'No,' Paige agreed, but she couldn't help admiring him for his commitment.

'In every way, I wanted to be the opposite to my father. I had a front-row seat to how his choices had made our family implode, had destroyed, in many ways, Luca's mother's life, and Luca's too. From the moment Lauren told me about Amanda, I was her father. It's as simple as that.'

It was impossible not to feel something like love for the sentiment he was expressing. It was exactly what she wished someone had felt for her. What had always been missing in her life. An ache throbbed in the back of her throat and she blinked away, hating the quick sting of tears in her eyes.

'Paige?' His voice was deep and husky, probing. She turned back to him slowly, her smile ambivalent, apologetic.

'I just never experienced that kind of love,' she said wistfully. 'I can't imagine what it must be like for Amanda to know that she has you.'

He was quiet, considered that. 'I'm the last person she seems to want to be around right now.'

Paige lifted her shoulders. 'Being a good dad isn't always about having the answers, it's about knowing how to get them. Your instincts were bang on: Amanda needs more right now. She needs a fresh perspective, and you're giving her that. Recognising that you have some shortcomings, that you can't fix everything, makes you brave and responsible. You're not letting her down.'

He hadn't said anything like it, but somehow, Paige just knew he needed to hear that. Perhaps it was a relic of the man Max had once been, the man who'd always needed to win.

Their meals arrived and they ate in between bursts of companionable conversation about the area, Max's family history here, and how much he loved this part of the world. He explained how it was his great-great-grandfather who'd moved to the north of Australia and opened a pearl-farming operation, that he'd been both lucky and canny, finding enormous pearls within his first five years of operation, some of which had been sold to the royal family for coronation jewels, and which quickly garnered a reputation as some of the most prestigious pearls in the world. From there, the operation had grown and successive generations had invested into other industries, had expanded their luxury holdings, so the Stone family was worth billions before being a billionaire was even a thing. But always, Wattle Bay and nearby Mamili had been special to them, because here it had all begun.

He painted such a picture and Paige was so pleasantly full of delicious prawns and lovely wine that she found herself relaxing back in the seat, listening and letting herself be pulled away by the richness of his history.

'I always wanted to live here. After Lauren died, I knew I needed to go back to basics. Lauren had loved the finer things in life, the fast pace, the luxury and glamour of Sydney, and our frequent trips overseas—whenever I suggested moving to Wattle Bay, she refused, told me I could come but not with her and not with our daughter.'

Paige gasped.

Max continued, 'She died because she went to some concert, got loaded backstage with the band, then let some equally drunk guy get behind the wheel of her ridiculous sports car. He wrapped the car around a pole. And suddenly I realised: my daughter can't grow up with any of this stuff. I don't want her going to schools with other rich kids, thinking it's normal to have an army of servants in the house, like I used to live, like Lauren lived. I didn't want her being chauffeur-driven in a Mercedes from one birthday party to the next, doing drugs at fifteen, in rehab by seventeen. It's as though Lauren's death forced me to grapple with the scaffolding of the world I was providing for Amanda. She was only five, so it wasn't too hard to strip away those luxuries, to bring her here, to the middle of nowhere, a home where she has to make her own bed and clear the table, where very few of those creature comforts infiltrate our world.'

'You don't take her away with you, if you travel for work?' Paige asked over the now cleared table. 'I presume your job requires you to leave the property?'

'Yes,' he agreed. 'Sometimes she comes with me, but most of the time, Amanda stays home, with Reg and his wife, Cass. They're great with her.'

'You don't think they could help, with her current moods?'

'They've raised five kids of their own,' he said fondly.

'They babysit their million grandkids in their off hours. I didn't particularly want to saddle them with my issues.'

'I've seen Reg with her. He's great. I'm sure he'd have been happy to help.'

'I needed more. I wanted proper support. Twenty-four-seven, help on tap. Hence, you're here.'

'Yes,' she agreed, nodding slowly. That was why she was here, and it was important not to forget that, even when they were inching closer and closer together, legs entwined beneath the table, heads close together, as though they were the only people in the pub. 'And you didn't consider a more permanent solution? Like hiring a nanny for the long term?'

He stiffened and Paige shook her head, worried he'd misinterpret. 'I don't mean that I want to stay,' she hastened to add, ignoring the awful pain in the centre of her heart at his quick and complete rejection of that idea.

He practically grunted his response. 'I was raised by nannies. An army of them. It's no way to live.'

She bowed her head forward. 'I thought I was the poster child for dysfunctional upbringings.'

'If it's any consolation, I think that's a prize you still get to keep.'

She blinked up at him and saw sympathy in his amazing eyes. Her fingers tingled with a need to touch him. She leaned closer, then let her hand lift, to his face, to his lips, tracing the outline as if committing it to memory.

'Would you like to see the dessert menu?' The waitress appeared, flicking a curious glance from one to the other.

Paige startled, surprised to find they were still in the middle of the pub.

'Paige?' Max's eyes were hungry, but not for dessert,

and it was a feeling that was reverberating inside Paige like a flag in a cyclone.

'I think we should go,' she said, eyes locked to his.

'I'm delighted to hear it. Put lunch on my tab, Clara.' He stood then reached for Paige, half pulling her out of her chair in his haste to exit the dining room.

Control was slipping away, inexorably and completely, as he pushed Paige's skirt up her body and dragged down her pants. He'd barely been able to wait until the helicopter door was closed and he'd never been so grateful that the chopper was a decent size *and* that it had darkly tinted windows. Confident they were screened off from anyone out there, and not much able to care beyond giving privacy a cursory thought, he pulled Paige down on top of him, as he had that first night in his office when his control had been dangling by a thread. Even then, he'd been powerless to fight this.

Lightning.

It had struck him again and again, always with Paige.

It had never been like this with Lauren. He didn't know why he'd said that it was. Maybe because it seemed wise to add in that kind of detail, some hint of self-preservation and guardedness? Or maybe because he'd actually believed it in that moment, but as Paige fumbled and finally undid his button and zip and released his rock-hard erection from his jeans, pausing only to take the condom from his wallet and sheathe him before lowering herself over his length with a loud, wrenching cry, he knew it had never been like this with anyone.

This was true lightning.

Life-changing, if you allowed it to be, but neither of them

would. So instead, they'd both just sit back and enjoy the ride, as many times as they possibly could before Paige's contract was up and she left.

CHAPTER TEN

AN EASY RHYTHM established itself. Amanda was Paige's sole focus whenever she was home from school and awake, and, to Paige's relief, Amanda continued to let Paige into her life, relaxing into conversations, even suggesting some shared activities like watching a movie together. But once Amanda was in bed and fast asleep, Paige was all Max's, and he was all hers. They used a guest room, far from the family's bedrooms, because it was imperative that Amanda should never have any possible hint of what was happening between the two of them.

It also seemed right to separate what they were doing from their normal lives. This was something they'd carved out that existed in its own space, away from the rest of their worlds.

In that room, Paige wasn't Paige and Max wasn't Max, they were just two people who found they came most to life when they were in each other's arms, bodies bonded, for those few hours each night before taking themselves back to their beds to wake up the next morning and resume the rhythm.

Strange, though, how after a week of this Paige felt simultaneously the most and least satisfied she'd ever been.

On the one hand, sex with Max was fulfilling and incredible, each time they came together somehow *more* wondrous than the last. She simply couldn't fathom how it could keep getting better.

But on the other hand, when it came time to say goodbye, she felt frustrated. A yearning was beginning to build inside Paige for the most ludicrous thing—particularly given the level of intimacy they'd shared.

What she really wanted though was to wake up beside him.

She wanted to see him sleep, to watch him wake, to be kissed awake by him—all impossible dreams, made just out of reach by the precarious nature of their situation and their overriding responsibility to do the right thing by Amanda.

And so it was that in the kitchen each morning they were back to their dance of the magnetic poles, skating around each other, maintaining a very safe distance at all times. They knew that if they happened to accidentally brush up against one another, sparks would fly that surely even Amanda wouldn't be able to miss.

It was almost a relief to leave each morning with Reg and Amanda, just so Paige could take some time to breathe, to unwind, before coming home and being alone with Max.

Their routine had even managed to push thoughts of her parents' book from Paige's mind—almost completely. There was still the odd moment when it burst into her brain, the knowledge that it was now published, on shelves, being read by people, and she would feel a visceral pain radiate through her chest, so she would clutch at her breast and breathe deeply until it passed and she remembered that she was here, that she was safe, far from the influence of the people who'd given her life and some of life's toughest lessons.

Here, there was just Max.

At first, they'd spent the days out. Doing things. Swimming. Exploring the oyster farm, so that Max could teach her about something that was so new to Paige. She'd known that pearls came from oyster shells, but hadn't understood quite what a laborious and careful process harvesting them was, particularly when done humanely, and, watching Max talk about it, she couldn't help but perceive his passion for the art of it.

But as the days went by, and the pressure between them built, eventually they reached a point where it was harder and harder to leave the house. Yes, the farm was fascinating and compelling, but it involved seeing other people and being out in public and neither relished that. Not when they could be alone.

The moment Paige returned from the school run, and the front door was closed, Max was there, pressing her against it and kissing her, his hands roaming her body as though they hadn't seen each other for years and years, as though a drought had been building and this, finally, were the storm come to quench the land. In reality, it had only been hours, and it shouldn't have been physically possible to want and need like this but, oh, how they did! She yearned for him on every level, and evidently he felt the same, because there was no restraint in their lovemaking. They were each as desperate as the other.

They often didn't make it upstairs to a bedroom. His office was closer, or there was the floor in the hallway. It didn't matter. So long as they found their way back to each other, the location didn't come into it.

Each day passed far too quickly. Paige had set an alarm on her phone, just so she didn't let time get away from her and forget to collect Amanda—a very real risk given the level of distraction Max presented.

Ten days after their new routine had begun, on a startlingly hot and humid afternoon, Paige went with Reg to collect Amanda, glowing from the inside out, pleasure bubbling inside her as anticipation built already, for later that night.

But when Amanda got in the car, slamming the door behind her, and burst into tears, every single thought of Max and romance fled from Paige's head.

'What's happened?' Paige asked, but Amanda sat there silently, staring out of the window, arms crossed, tears leaking from her eyes and rolling slowly down her cheeks. It felt like a torturously slow drive home but finally Reg pulled the car into the drive and Amanda bolted out the moment he came to a stop, running up the steps and inside without a backwards glance.

'I— Thank you,' Paige murmured, face pale as she stepped from the car and walked towards the house, tossing over possibilities in her mind, trying to imagine what could possibly have happened.

Max stood in the door to his office, and even then, when their eyes met, Paige felt a crackle of electric energy fire through her blood. She ignored it.

'Amanda—'

'I saw. Why?'

Paige shook her head. 'I don't know.'

He sighed heavily. 'I'll go talk to her.'

Paige put out her hand. 'I'll go.' She squeezed his hand with her own. 'Let me try. I just have a feeling this is something I can help with. Do you mind?'

He looked uncertain but, after a few moments, nodded. When she went to pull away though, he flipped his hand, easily capturing hers in his. 'She can be fierce when she's in these moods. Don't let her get to you.'

Paige's heart skipped a beat. 'Max Stone, are you actually being protective of me?'

Something shifted in his eyes—surprise? And then guardedness, as he lifted one shoulder half defensively. 'Just a warning.'

'Consider me warned,' she said gently. Again, she tried to move away but, instead of letting go, he pulled her closer and pressed the lightest of kisses to the tip of her nose.

After everything they'd shared, all their intimacies, it was this kiss that had the power to take her breath away and make her toes and fingers tingle, to steal her breath, all her breath, and give her knees the shakes.

'Good luck.' He pulled back then, putting physical space between them but also changing his stature completely so he was somehow stronger, more imposing, less familiar to her.

Paige simply smiled, careful not to show any of her thoughts. 'Fingers crossed.'

Much later that night, having eaten a quiet dinner alone with Amanda in the downstairs play area, and shared a real, meaningful conversation with her about what had been going on in Amanda's life, Paige finally understood, and knew she needed to explain to Max.

'She's being teased,' Paige said gently, curled up on the daybed on the veranda, so close to Max she was practically in his lap. It was late. Amanda had been asleep for over an hour, and Max and Paige were in their favourite place, outside, staring up at the starlit sky accompanied by the orchestra of night birds and the rolling, crashing waves of the ocean. Every sense came alive inside Paige out here; being this close to Max supercharged it all.

'Teased?' He responded quickly, loudly, his body tensing in a way Paige felt. 'What the actual hell? By whom?'

'Just some girls at school,' Paige murmured. 'It's not uncommon at this age. I've emailed her teacher and headmistress. I'm going to meet with them to discuss it, but it sounds reasonably benign—'

'Benign, my ass. You've seen her moods. Are you telling me that's because some awful girls are taking their own self-esteem issues out on Amanda?'

Paige pressed a hand to his chest. 'I know you're upset, but, believe it or not, this is not as bad as it sounds.'

He scowled at her, and his defensiveness made Paige's chest feel as if a thousand tonnes of cement were being pushed against it. On the one hand, she loved that this was his reaction, but she couldn't help thinking again of the absences she'd felt in her own life, how, when she was a teenager, she'd desperately needed protecting. And there'd been no one.

'How exactly is it not so bad?' he drawled, and while she knew his anger wasn't aimed at her, it still hurt. They were a team, fighting through this together.

'Conflict in life is inevitable.'

'Is this conflict? Or is she being bullied?'

Paige stroked his chest, changing her description as a concession to his point. 'Unpleasantness is a part of life. We all have to learn to deal with cruel people, unfair situations, and the more we do it with the support and guidance of trusted adults, the better we become at managing those situations independently. Think of yourself—and me—as her training wheels. We're here to help Amanda learn how to stand up for herself, to find her voice, and to draw her own boundaries of what is and isn't acceptable. By going through this now, the next time something like this happens—and it will, because that's life—she'll be better able to cope.'

He ground his teeth together. 'Who the hell are these kids?'

'A couple of girls in her grade, and a few in the grade above. I think two of them are sisters,' she said. 'I couldn't quite keep up, but I'll get a clearer picture once I've met with her teacher and headmistress—which I'll be doing tomorrow.'

'Like hell you will.'

'Max—'

'Paige, with respect, Amanda is your job. She's my daughter. Obviously I should be the one to sort this out.'

Paige flinched. While his statement was accurate, it was also cruel, and it cut right down to the middle of her chest. Had she lost sight of her role here? Of the fact she was the hired help? Dispensable. Disposable. Just like always. Unconsciously, she pulled away a little, putting some physical distance between them to echo the emotional wedge he'd thrust into the space.

'That's exactly why you shouldn't.' Her voice was hoarse. She cleared her throat, ignoring her pain, knowing she could analyse and explore it later. 'You're too emotionally involved. Try to remember, the other girls who are in this are also just getting their training wheels, learning how to interact. The situation doesn't need hot-headed grown-ups racing down there pointing fingers. It's a learning experience. In the first instance, the girls should be encouraged to do better. If they don't, if this keeps happening, then you might want to consider upping the ante.'

'I can't believe this. I will pull her out of the school and—'

'And what?' Paige asked with genuine curiosity. 'Where would you send her?'

He hesitated.

'There are kids who make bad choices at every school. The only thing you can control is how Amanda manages herself, by teaching her resilience and perspective. Don't overreact.'

'What the hell are they teasing her about, anyway? There's never been a better kid, for Christ's sake.'

Paige dipped her head forward to hide her smile, but it was a watery smile, because again and again he demonstrated his love for his daughter, his total love, and the contrast with how Paige had been raised never failed to hit her right between the eyes.

'Well…' She hesitated, aware that the next statement would seem like a criticism. 'Actually, it really started off with swimming lessons,' Paige said softly.

'That was a couple of months ago.'

She nodded. 'Apparently Amanda was the only girl who didn't have a two-piece.'

'A two-piece? You mean a bikini?' He stared at Paige incredulously.

'Amanda says she got her bathers when she was much younger.'

'Right. Reg and Cass gave them to her.' He looked genuinely baffled. 'But she never said she wanted anything else. They still fit.'

Paige nodded sympathetically. 'Yes, they do, but they're bright pink with a neon yellow frill.'

'What's wrong with that?'

Paige put a hand on his knee, and avoided getting into an explanation of how young the bathers seemed to the other girls. 'And then, one of the girls came back after the holidays wearing a trainer bra, and all the other girls followed suit.'

'A trainer bra? They're kids!'

'Kids,' she said, 'are growing up faster and faster all the time. For this generation, that's normal.'

His Adam's apple shifted visibly as he swallowed.

'Paige was too embarrassed to ask you. For the bikini, or the bra.'

'Too embarrassed?' he repeated, then swore, dragging a hand through his hair and carefully dislodging Paige so he could stand, pacing to the edge of the veranda and bracing his hands around the railing. He cursed again. 'What the hell have I been doing wrong, Paige?' He turned to face her, his eyes haunted, and she knew he wasn't really seeing her, but was rather replaying every parenting moment of the last few years.

'Nothing,' Paige was quick to insist. She stood, moving towards him, wrapping her arms around his waist and pressing herself against him so she could feel the solid, if faster than normal, beating of his heart. 'This is *normal*. Girls—and boys, but more often girls—are jostling for social dominance. It's awful and hard to watch but it's *normal*. And short of pulling Amanda out of school altogether and completely curating her life for her—which is a fast track to failure because she'll emerge as an adult with no coping skills—you really can't do anything except what you're doing. And what you're doing so, so well, Max. I mean that. You love her. You clearly love her, so much, and she knows it. Nothing, nothing, nothing is going to build her up better than understanding that, no matter what happens at school, she can come home to you, that everything will be okay because you're here.'

He tilted his face away, a muscle jerking in the base of his jaw, emotion radiating off him. Tears filmed Paige's eyes. 'You're a really great dad.' The strength of her feelings was a sinkhole, threatening to pull her in. She needed levity, something to help lighten the mood. 'And I'm not just saying that because you're amazing in bed.'

He turned back to her, eyes heavy when they met Paige's, but then he was smiling, and she smiled back, a melancholy smile laced with all the emotions that were rioting through her, that she hoped he wasn't able to see.

'Thank you.' He paused, lifting a hand and stroking her hair. Tingles spread through Paige like wildfire. His voice grew gravelled. 'On both counts.'

Paige pressed her head to his chest, listening to his heart. His hand stroked her hair, but it was his next words that made Paige feel a thousand and one things.

'I'm sorry no one ever loved you like that, Paige. I'm sorry your parents let you down so badly.'

Her heart stammered. She closed her eyes, hoping to push away the strange feeling that was stealing through her: that he was giving her something she'd always needed, a form of salvation that shouldn't have been his to offer. 'It's fine.'

'It's not fine. Hearing you talk about them, what you've told me, what they did to you—you deserved so much better. I think it's a miracle that you're such a patient, kind and loving person.'

But Paige wasn't loving. He was wrong. It often took all of her concentration to ensure she didn't slip up, that she didn't accidentally let herself love. For while she cared a great deal about her clients, and loved looking after children, she was always careful not to let love enter the equation.

'Thank you,' she said, quietly, because there was no sense reminding him of that now. She took the praise and buried it in a special part of her brain, for the very few memories she possessed that she liked to revisit, time and again.

'I just didn't want her to be like Lauren,' he said with a shake of his head, staring at the sand beneath his feet, phone to his ear.

'I know, man.' As always, Luca's voice was comforting, because Luca *knew* what Max was up against. He'd been there for the absolute disaster that had been their marriage. He'd seen Lauren's excesses, the destruction, he'd heard Max's worries about it even then.

'This was an epic ball-drop though. I mean, how did I not realise she always wears the same goddamned bathers? And she probably only even has that pair because Reg and Cass realised what she was missing and stepped in to help.'

'She has bathers. She has clothes. A roof over her head. And you're way more present in her life than Carrick was in ours.'

Guilt washed over Max. It hadn't been his fault, but whenever they compared their childhoods, he felt bad for how neglected Luca had been. Not that coming to live with their father had been any better.

'Besides, this is an easy fix.'

'Yeah?'

'Take her shopping,' Luca said with a quiet laugh. 'Not just shopping. Take her to Sydney. Hell, take her overseas. In fact, I've got a great idea.'

'Oh, yeah? I'm all ears,' Max muttered, in disbelief that he hadn't tweaked as to what might have been going on.

'Singapore has the best boutiques—at least, according to Mia.' Affection softened Luca's voice when he referred to his wife, clearly the love of Luca's life. 'I've got to go there this weekend to check on one of my developments. Come meet me. I'll bring Mia and the kids. They'd love to see you both. And you can spoil Amanda. Send her back to school with the kind of stuff those other girls will go crazy for.'

'I'm not going to make her think she has to earn their approval,' Max responded quickly. 'Amanda's great. She's just lacking a few of the essentials.'

'Sure, but if you've overlooked those, then imagine what else she probably needs. She's almost a teenager, Max. It's not just about what's practical. She must want some clothes that are actually, you know, fashionable.'

'Sydney has good shops.' But at the same time, a chance to see Luca, Mia and the kids was hard to resist.

Max hesitated. Despite his misgivings that any kind of shopping spree now could be seen as a validation of the bullies' attitudes, his brother was right. Max had been getting Reg and Cass to organise clothes for Paige for almost as long as he'd been living out this way. And while she always had T-shirts and shorts, maybe she had reached an age and stage where she wanted dresses. Heaven help him, shoes with little heels? Handbags? He felt sweat break out on his brow as he stared down the barrel of raising an actual teenager, all on his own.

Something heavy lodged in the back of his mind, a feeling he couldn't quite make sense of. But when he thought about raising Amanda, weirdly, Paige was somehow threaded into that idea, as though she might be able to offer an alternative, more lasting support. Just as she had that night after they'd slept together, when he'd looked at Paige and his daughter cooking together and felt a weird sense of having come home.

But he wasn't about to outsource the parenting of his child, nor to start to rely on anyone else when it came to raising Amanda. Paige was amazing. A great addition to their lives, but she was temporary. He had to continue to navigate this mostly on his own.

'Okay. We'll come to you.' He frowned, thinking instantly of Paige, and what it would mean to travel with her, of how the life they'd forged at each other's sides would have to be put on hold for the next few days.

'You'll stay in the apartment with us?'

Max immediately dismissed that idea. Luca's luxury apartment was in a prime Singapore location with stunning views and Max generally stayed with Luca when he was in town, but it lacked privacy. In a hotel room—a large hotel penthouse—he could at least still get time alone with Paige when Amanda went to bed, just as they did here. Staying in the same apartment as Luca, Mia and their children, he'd feel as though it was impossible to slip away, and there was no way Mia would miss the signs of what was going on between him and Paige, and then there'd be a thousand questions and he was afraid he didn't have any answers. When he thought about what he was doing, the truth was, he simply didn't know.

'No.' He sought an excuse quickly. 'If I'm going to spoil her, I'm going to completely spoil her, just for one weekend—I'll book a suite at the Ashworth. I'll text you details once we take off. See you soon, Luca.'

He disconnected the call with a new-found sense of purpose.

Max, a man of action, was simply relieved that there was *something* he could do to make his daughter's life better, and to atone for having failed to realise that her needs were changing as she grew up.

But he could—and would—fix that.

And getting to share Singapore with Paige? a little voice in his head taunted.

Max grinned.

Better and better.

CHAPTER ELEVEN

IT HAD BEEN a stupid idea, Max thought with a scowl, at the end of a long day spent being close to Paige but unable to touch her. And, worse, she was annoyed at him. He didn't know why, but suspected she thought this whole idea was stupid too. Maybe she had a foresight he lacked, or maybe his initial instinct had been correct—that he was somehow teaching Amanda to bend to bullies.

He sure as hell didn't enjoy being crammed into his private jet—which had never felt small before, but with Paige and Amanda playing cards across the aisle, Paige's sleeve dropping down over her shoulder as she laughed so he ached to reach across and fix it, to brush his fingers over her bare flesh, to reach for her chin and tilt her face to his, to kiss her petal-soft lips. But he hadn't. He'd sat in his chair, like a block of ice, working, reading, staring straight ahead and willing away the hours into Singapore.

It was a seven-hour flight, so when Amanda fell asleep he'd had some hope that Paige might shift across to sit with him, or, better yet, suggest they move to a private cabin, but Paige drifted off almost as soon as Amanda had, leaving Max awake, alone, trying to concentrate but finding that near impossible with Paige across the aisle and so beautiful in sleep.

He realised he'd never seen her like this.

Sleeping.

Lips parted slightly, lashes so dark against her pale skin, hair pulled over one shoulder so again, his fingers ached to reach over and brush through it. Her shirt stayed loose, dropped down on one side.

His mouth went dry and his body tightened, every muscle on alert, hopeful, wishing...

He consoled himself with the knowledge they'd touch down soon, that the presidential suite he'd booked at the prestigious harbourfront hotel would offer more than enough space and privacy for him and Paige to be together.

Except it hadn't turned out that way.

Paige had settled Amanda into her room—after the flight and waking up for the drive into the city, Amanda was disorientated and a little upset, so it took Paige longer to get her settled, and then she'd evidently fallen asleep in Amanda's room, leaving Max with nothing to do but go to his own room and hope Paige woke at some point and came to him...

Only, she didn't.

The next day was spent shopping for Paige and Amanda, and in meetings with Luca. They inspected Luca's development, as well as the flagship Stone store in Singapore, and for some reason Max found it almost impossible not to talk to Luca about Paige.

Not about their relationship, just *about* her. About her life, her smile, her hair, how good she was for Amanda, how much of a difference she'd made to their lives. He found he wanted to talk about the small things, but instead, he was silent.

They ate dinner as a family.

Luca and Mia, their kids, and Amanda and Max.

No Paige. 'There's no need to include me,' she'd whispered to him, eyes flashing, so the first wave of misgivings began to form in his gut as he realised she was potentially avoiding him on purpose, rather than just owing to the circumstances of their trip.

By the time he and Amanda came home, he'd reached the end of his rope.

He missed her.

Not just physically, but all of her. He missed sitting on the veranda listening to the ocean and talking to her. He missed hearing about her day, listening to her speak about the kids she'd raised and her experiences in Dubai, and sometimes, when she was feeling particularly brave, her parents. He just *missed her*.

It should have served as a warning to end things, because at some point Paige would be gone for good and he'd have to get on with normal life, as it had been before.

And he would, he reassured himself quickly, determined not to worry about something he wouldn't allow to become a problem.

Besides, by the time Paige had to leave, he'd have worked her out of his system. It was just the newness of this. The connecting with someone after a period of such isolation and celibacy. Of course that was drugging and hypnotic. It wasn't really about Paige at all, so much as how pleasant it was to have another adult in his life to share things with.

Temporarily.

Only right now, that other adult was doing her level best to avoid him, and he was fed up with it.

Max Stone was not a man to be ignored.

Growing up, Paige had been surrounded by luxury, from the hotels she'd stayed at on location to the Hills home her parents had bought. But this was a whole other level. From the private jet to the limousine that had brought them through the stunning, modern city of Singapore and to this old-fashioned hotel on the harbour, to the presidential suite that was brimming with grandeur and classic elegance. It was also enormous, boasting four huge bedrooms, each with their own palatial bathroom, a ten-person dining table in the intimidatingly formal dining room, a small home cinema, a state-of-the-art kitchen and plush lounge room. There were several balconies, each boasting glorious views of the city in one direction and the water the other, so every angle held a feast for the eyes.

It was a level of decadence that Paige might have enjoyed if it weren't for her frustration with Max.

She knew what he was doing, and why. This was a knee-jerk reaction to what had happened with Amanda at school, and she supposed it was understandable that he'd respond this way. He could afford to, and there was no harm that could come from it. Probably. At least, not to Amanda.

But for Paige, it was the absolute opposite of what she'd wanted.

She'd taken the assignment in the far-flung Australian outback to get away from this sort of built-up civilisation. She'd wanted to be as removed as possible from the tabloids and TV shows, from the possibility of being recognised, of seeing herself on a book cover.

And instead, he'd brought her into the lion's den.

Which he had every right to do.

When she'd accepted this job, she hadn't specified an aversion to travel. This had been reasonably foreseeable, in fact, given Max's situation. She'd often accompanied families on holiday. And until now, that hadn't been such a troublesome concept. But Paige wanted, desperately, to hide out. To hide away.

And on the farm, in his tree house, she'd come to feel safe.

With just Max and Amanda forming the walls of her world, she'd felt in control of who she was, of how she was perceived.

This trip put her right out there again. Max probably hadn't even noticed but Paige had been horribly aware of lingering stares, of people looking at her today, wondering where they'd seen her, just as Max had. She felt more exposed than she'd been in years, all because of Max.

It was a blessing that no one had actually come up to her and asked if she was Aria Gray, but that didn't mean some enterprising person hadn't used their phone to snap a picture, which they'd on-sell to a tabloid paper, and the media frenzy would begin again, but worse, because she'd been with Max and Amanda and the possibility of their being linked would add so much fuel to the fire. All Paige wanted was a quiet life—and she would never have that if she was in a job that would involve this kind of trip.

She curled her fingers around the railing, breathing in the humid, tropical air, wishing with all that she was that she was back in Australia, or, really, anywhere other than this.

Misgiving swirled inside her and she couldn't quite put her finger on *why* she should be so annoyed with Max. True, he'd thrown her into a situation she'd specifically wished to avoid, but this was still Paige's job. He hadn't asked her to do anything outside the bounds of normal nannying work. He had simply been acting in what he perceived to be Amanda's best interests.

And not Paige's.

Realisation dawned and Paige made a little noise of surprise.

He had booked this trip without considering Paige. She'd told him about her life, her parents, the book, why she'd taken a job on the edges of the earth, and he'd booked this trip anyway.

He hadn't thought about how this might affect her.

And why should he have?

They were just sleeping together. They'd both been abundantly clear on that score. Why should he factor in Paige's needs at all? Let alone allow her needs to influence his plans? That would speak to a more significant relationship, to his actually *caring* about her; and that wasn't what their relationship was.

She swallowed past a wretched lump in her throat, surprised at how deep that wound went, at how his actions had been able to cut her deeply.

Worry began to fray the edges of her mind.

Worry because her whole philosophy in life was predicated on emotional detachment, on having the ability to control her connections to people and walk away whenever she needed to.

What if that was in jeopardy now?

She'd become good at caring for children without letting them claw too deep inside her heart. She clearly delineated what she did—as a job—and while she gave herself to it one hundred per cent, she never forgot her place, never forgot that she'd be moving on.

Something about Amanda was different though.

She was sweet, and hurt, and vulnerable, and Paige had needed to work hard to really tighten a bond with her, to earn Amanda's trust. But it was more than that.

When Paige looked at Amanda, she saw Max as well. His eyes, his stubborn temperament, his strength. She saw so many of the traits that were also in Max and those traits made her feel... She searched for the right word, shaking her head, exasperated when she couldn't properly untangle her emotions. Only she knew she did *feel* something, and that alone was anathema to her approach to life.

If she didn't care about Max, his lack of consideration of Paige's feelings wouldn't have rankled so much. But she did care, so it did hurt like hell.

With a soft groan, she spun to move inside, right as Max appeared at the wide French doors, stepping out onto the small balcony. His expression was impossible to misinterpret, his features locked in a mask that showed irritation and impatience, his eyes holding a warning. Paige, in the midst of desperately trying to fathom her own reactions, wished he would disappear again. It was all too much—the sense of overwhelm was huge.

'You're home?'

'We've been home twenty minutes. Amanda's asleep.'

Paige blinked. 'I didn't hear you come in.'

'Obviously.'

'Why didn't you come and get me? I would have liked to see Amanda. To say goodnight to her.'

'To take refuge in your duties to her, you mean? To hide from me again?'

Paige felt as though she'd been shocked with live voltage. 'I didn't—I don't know what you're talking about.'

'Come on, Paige. It's just the two of us now. Be honest with me. Why are you avoiding me?'

'I'm just doing my job,' she pointed out, the ground beneath her unsteady, because his accusation was justified and she didn't think it would be possible to explain what she was feeling without revealing something important—to herself, and him. She needed space to work out what was going on, damn it.

'You were doing your job back in Australia too,' he pointed out huskily, 'but you were also available to me.'

'Available to you?' she repeated, his choice of phrasing rubbing her completely the wrong way.

Something shifted in his eyes. Doubt? Uncertainty? Remorse? But it disappeared again quickly, the emotion replaced with arrogant certainty. 'We were both available to each other,' he conceded, arms crossed over his chest. 'What's changed?'

She turned away from him, staring out at the view, the beauty of the setting at odds with the turmoil inside her.

Realisations were coming at Paige like a runaway train and she couldn't move out of its path. Her head was spinning. She wanted to curl up under a rock, to run away and hide.

'I don't know what you're talking about,' she muttered.

'Oh, yeah?'

She did her best to feign innocence. 'Have I done something wrong with Amanda?'

'This isn't about—God, this isn't a job evaluation, Paige. I'm not talking about Amanda. I'm talking about us.'

Us. The train was screeching closer, the lights blinding, the clarity so close Paige could almost reach out and grab it, comprehension of her deepest feelings within grasp. But whenever she felt as if she was coming to understand herself, something shifted, morphed, so she no longer knew what she was feeling.

But the word 'us' sparked danger in her blood. She wasn't a part of an 'us', she never had been and she didn't ever intend to be.

'I think we've made a mistake,' she said slowly, but with firm resolve. 'Amanda has to be our priority.'

'She *is* our priority. I'm not criticising the way you are with her.'

Paige swallowed past a throat that seemed lined with razor blades. Everything was wrong. Flashes of their time together blinded Paige, bursting into her consciousness.

She'd been so confident—arrogant—assured that she could control this, and all the while something about Max had weaved deep into her soul. And Amanda had done exactly the same thing, in a way no other child Paige had been charged with the responsibility of had managed.

Despite her best intentions, something about this pair

had been too impossible to resist and she'd come to really care for them. To rely on them. To want them in her life.

So much so that the thought of leaving in a little over two months' time made her heart turn to ice.

It was one too many departures.

One too many goodbyes.

A single tear rolled down her cheek and she was so grateful her back was turned, that she was staring, troubled, out at the bay, rather than facing Max and this disaster head-on.

'For God's sake, Paige. Have I done something to hurt you?' There was desperation in his plea, as though hurting her would be the worst thing in the world.

She closed her eyes on a wave of unmitigated sadness. He really had no idea. And why should he? Nothing in his behaviour had been at fault. He had every right to book this trip, to expect his child's nanny to accompany him. He had every damned right.

The problem wasn't Max, it was Paige. She'd started to want more from him than he'd ever offered, to want the same protectiveness he gave Amanda to extend around Paige too. In the middle of the mess that was her personal life, she'd wanted Max to wrap his broad arms around her, to care for her, to show her that she could actually trust someone else with her heart, and even her life. She'd wanted him to realise the risks and discomfort to Paige, in joining him on this trip, and to factor that into his plans. To think about her, not as a nanny, or someone he was sleeping with, but as a woman he truly cared about.

He'd failed her, and he didn't even realise it, because her expectations were so wildly out of step with the reality of their dynamic. He'd failed her by not being what she needed—and she hated that she needed anything from him at all. He hadn't done anything wrong, and yet he'd hurt her.

Paige had come to Australia to run away from her old life, and now she wanted to run away from what she'd found in Australia: her own fallibility.

Her heart was vulnerable.

She was capable of loving, of wanting to be loved. It had just taken the right person—people—to make her see that.

'Damn it.' He was right behind her, his hands on her arms, turning her to face him, his eyes raking over her face, desperate to see, to understand, to know what had upset her, but Paige couldn't answer him, because all the answers were flying at her thick and fast and it was an answer she could never give him anyway, because she'd broken faith: she'd promised him she could be trusted, that everything would be fine, and, in the end, she'd lied.

Because despite what she'd told him, Paige loved Max.

Looking up into his eyes now, she saw it as clear as day. Every kiss, every moment, every conversation that had bared her soul to him and vice versa, Paige had been falling unknowingly in love.

It shocked and terrified her.

She lifted a hand to her lips, pressing it there, her eyes smarting from the tears she was desperately trying to hold in check.

'Paige?' But he was angry now, frustrated with not being able to understand. 'Has something happened? Is there something more going on? Is it the book?'

She shook her head quickly. 'It was the book. Sort of. I was—I was—'

'You were what?'

He groaned, and he was so close to her, so achingly close, that everything seemed both complicated and simple at the same time.

'Just—forget about it,' she whispered, lifting up onto her tiptoes and kissing him. It was a kiss that obliterated thought and sense and all the parameters of the world as Paige had perceived them because she *felt* love. She felt it radiate through her body, permeate her soul, fundamentally change who she was. She was losing herself, just as she'd always been terrified of, but she didn't know if she minded, she only knew she couldn't stop. Not then. She couldn't walk away from him. From this.

It was all her worst fears come to bear but surrendering now was also the most sublime form of completion she'd ever, ever known.

It didn't sound, on paper, like something that should have bothered him, but the next morning, with Paige back to ignoring him, Max couldn't shake the feeling she'd used sex to avoid having a heavier conversation. That rather than explain to him why she was upset, she'd pushed their chemistry to the fore, and he'd let her. Hell, he'd needed her. He'd been driven mindless with missing her, wanting her. They'd made love and it had been so perfect, different, somehow, from before, perhaps because of whatever was going on with her. Or maybe it was because he'd had to reckon with how much he loved being with Paige when she'd become unavailable to him; her absence had made him grapple with how used to her he'd become. When she'd pulled away, he hadn't enjoyed it.

But they had more than two months left before her contract ended and, far from resenting the necessity of a nanny, he was praying his thanks to every god that existed for the fact she'd be with them for so long.

They would fly back to Australia the following day, and everything would go back to normal. It was the thought he comforted himself with throughout the day, whenever he'd look at Paige and she'd determinedly avoid making eye contact with him.

Everything would be normal again soon. He didn't want to analyse why that thought reassured him so much…

Paige's fingers shook as she sent the email, and the moment it whooshed out of the computer and into the ether her stomach dropped to her toes and she angsted over whether she'd just made a colossal mistake.

She was running away again.

She was scared, and she was leaving, because she didn't know how to stay and fight. Because she couldn't. She couldn't fight for a future with Max. He'd told her it wasn't possible, and while she might have *hoped* he'd changed his mind, as she had, she couldn't bear to think of what his rejection would feel like. Another rejection, but this one so much worse than any other. It would be the straw that broke the camel's back—or at least, broke Paige.

And so she would leave.

It would hurt like hell at first, but once she managed to put some distance between herself and this place, from Max and Amanda, and even bloody Reg, Paige would start to feel more like herself. She just needed, desperately, to get away.

CHAPTER TWELVE

MAX STARED AT his computer screen with the sensation the bottom had just fallen out of his world.

Dear Mr Stone,

I regret to inform you that for personal reasons Ms Cooper will no longer be able to continue with her contract. While such occurrences are rare, from time to time we do find our staff members' situations change for reasons beyond our control. Please accept my most sincere apologies for this. Ms Cooper has advised that her last day will be in one week.

I have attached the profiles of three different nannies who would be available immediately to replace Ms Cooper.

Please advise which staff member you would like to engage when you've had a chance to review their CVs, and if I can help with anything in the meantime, please do not hesitate to be in touch.

Best wishes
Nicholas Tankard, CEO

'What the actual hell?' he snapped into the air of his study, flicking his laptop down and scraping back his chair, staring at the door for about three seconds before prowling over to it and pulling it open as if the thing had done him some great personal wrong.

What the actual hell?

The house was silent except for the sound of his rough breathing.

He stormed from room to room, throwing open the doors, his mood worsening with each room he looked into and found empty.

At the back door of the house, he stared out, frowning mutinously at the darkening sky, the heat of the day sticky and oppressive, but he barely noticed any of those things. He was focused on Paige with a singular intensity.

He took the old timber stairs—rarely used—onto the lawn at the rear of the house, stalking past an enormous, ancient frangipani tree, a threadbare blanket of the tree's first flowers starting to brown at the edges. Max trampled them without noticing.

On the edges of the lawn was the rainforest, and a throwaway comment Paige had made a few days before Singapore reverberated through his mind. *'I'd love to explore it. I'll have to, before I go.'* At the time, he'd dismissed it, because of *course* there'd be time for that. He hadn't realised that she'd already been planning an early departure.

He ground his teeth, step quickening, sky darkening behind him. By the time he reached the edge of the rainforest, the first of the big, fat raindrops had begun to fall and the petrichor was instantly familiar to Max, who'd grown up with these sorts of tropical storms.

'Paige?' he shouted, anger tangling with worry now as he mentally catalogued the number of things that could go wrong in the rainforest for someone lacking experience. From snakes to spiders to leeches to slippery rocks, lantana, dangerous edges, fallen branches. 'Paige?' His voice ripped through the moss-covered tree trunks as he went deeper and deeper, his gut churning for a thousand reasons, none of them good.

She woke as if from a long, long sleep, eyes heavy, head fuzzy, and the first thing she noticed was that the light was so magical—almost green—and then, she heard it again. Her name, loud yet muffled. Standing, she moved to the edge of the attic where a small window showed a bird's eye view of this tropical paradise. Her heart twisted because she wouldn't be here for much longer to appreciate this stunning vista. She would always remember this place though; it was here that she'd realised something about herself she'd thought impossible. She wasn't so utterly destroyed that she couldn't love.

It scared her but, on another level, it also gave her hope.

Maybe, maybe this meant her future would be different from the grim one she'd always anticipated.

Except…how?

She'd felt love here, but it was love for Max and Amanda, for this place. Despite what Max had said, Paige didn't believe lightning would strike twice.

This alone was it.

When she left, her heart would remain behind.

Always.

'Paige?'

There was something in his voice, something awfully, blood-curdlingly panicked, so she was running before she realised it, out of the attic door and down the old narrow stairs, to the next level of this magical house, then down the next stairs, and the next, then out of the front door, onto the lawn, where she paused, panting, hands on hips as she waited, listening—where was he? Rain fell, heavy, and out to sea a blade of lightning sliced through the thick, leaden sky. A moment later, thunder rolled, so loud it vibrated in the pit of Paige's stomach.

And then, another sound—his voice, and from out here she could distinguish its direction: the rainforest.

She ran to the edges. Worry slicked her palms with sweat; at the barrier of the rainforest, it was much darker and cooler. The canopy was so thick it effectively blotted out almost all of the light, and the trunks were covered in lichen and moss and strange, green vines that almost looked to be strangling some of the thicker trees—she'd seen these in the photograph in Max's office.

She stepped across the threshold and amongst the trunks, peering into the forest.

His voice came again.

'What is it? Max?' she called, lifting her hand to her eyes to block the falling rain. Strangely though, the same roof of leaves that prevented light also slowed the rain, so only the odd drop got through.

Silence.

Worry built in her gut.

Where was he? She moved in deeper, but it was so dark, and the path had craggy rocks everywhere. 'Where are you?'

She stood still, listening, but all she heard in response was the call of a whip bird, and the splatter of raindrops—

more now, as the weight on the leaves gave them a downward tilt.

'Jesus Christ, Paige, where were you?' He came almost out of nowhere, like a spirit conjured by this magical jungle of a place. But it wasn't a spirit, it was Max, her Max.

She closed her eyes, bracing herself for reality: he wasn't hers and never would be.

'What's wrong? What's the matter?'

'You don't ever come in here alone—do you understand that? This is not a safe place.'

She stared at him, confused, but there was so much emotion in his face, his eyes, the tightness around his lips, that she struggled to know how to respond. 'I only came in here because you were calling for me,' she said, eventually, shivering without knowing why. Despite the rain, it wasn't cold. The air was thick with humidity.

'What's happened?' she asked, wrapping her arms around her chest.

His eyes bored through her soul, lancing her with their intensity; Paige's shivering intensified.

'Would you care to explain this?' He reached into his back pocket and withdrew his phone, his hand slightly unsteady as he paused, scanning the screen before holding it up for her to see.

Her heart dropped to her toes. Paige had asked her boss to let *her* tell Max and Amanda. Evidently keeping the client happy was more important than looking after his staff.

'I can explain,' she whispered, lifting a hand to his chest, pressing it there, almost falling to her knees at how close she was to his rapidly beating heart, at her desperation for that heart to beat for her.

'Can you?' he demanded, stepping away from her, so Paige's hand dropped into the air between them. 'Give it a shot, then.'

She swallowed, brows drawing together, at a loss for words because, actually, *could* she explain? How could she tell him that she'd fallen in love with him?

She stared up at Max, mouth gaping, then shook her head. 'I have to go.'

His eyes flashed with so much anger that she almost did a double take. This version of Max was completely foreign to her. She'd never seen him physically reverberating with emotion before. A glimmer of hope lifted inside her, because if he was this angry, maybe it meant he did actually care?

Or maybe it meant his ego was smarting, she thought. Or that he was irritated at her reneging on their contract. Those options were far more likely.

She tried to remember what she'd planned to tell him, back when she'd put this plan in motion. A sanitised version of her thoughts that made it all so calm and rational.

'With everything going on in my personal life right now,' she began, haltingly, 'with the book, I just need to take some time to myself. I'm sure you can understand—'

'You want space?' He dragged a hand through his hair. 'Fine. Have your space. But stay here. You can still work for me. Be with Amanda. You and I don't have to continue our personal relationship.'

She closed her eyes, pain lashing her, because he said that so immediately and with such ease, as if he could simply flick a switch and shut down what they were doing. For Paige, there was just no way. If they were living in this house together, she'd be overwhelmed by her need for him, by her love for him. She'd want things that weren't, and never would be, possible.

'It's not that easy,' she whispered, the words almost completely drowned out by the forest.

'To hell it isn't. You're making it complicated.'

She gaped. 'How, exactly?'

'You said you came here to hide out. To get away from that damned book. So what's changed?' he demanded, crossing his arms over his chest and staring down at her. The sound of falling rain was like the quickening of a drum, perfectly echoing the fast pace of her heart.

'Where are you going to go next, Paige? Antarctica?'

She flinched. He was so angry!

'Amanda needs you,' he said with quiet disgust, so her heart turned to ice. Amanda needed her. That was true, but it was also hurtful, because Paige wanted to be needed by Max too.

'I know,' she whispered, pressing a hand to her chest. *I need her too.* 'But she has you. She's doing better now. She'll be okay.'

'You tell yourself that if it's what you need to believe, but the truth is you're running away for your own selfish needs and, in the process, you're letting down a little girl who relies on you.'

She gasped and staggered backwards, one step, so angry, so hurt, so desperately, achingly sore. 'How dare you?'

'How dare *I*?' He glared at her. 'You're kidding, right?'

They stared at each other across the chasm of their emotions, the air pulsing with hurt, betrayal and a million unspoken words.

'You are incredible,' he said, shaking his head. 'I can't believe I ever thought—' The words stopped. He frowned, silenced, mid-sentence.

'You thought what?' Everything hinged on his response. Anticipation stretched, desperate, intense, in the very centre of her chest. The noises of the forest took on an almost deafening quality—crickets, rain, whip birds, a stream.

'That you were the answer to our prayers.' He spun around and stalked out of the forest, but at the edge, he stopped, hands on hips, staring a little way in, evidently waiting for Paige, who could barely think over the cacophony of her rushing blood.

'What does that even mean?' she shouted, making her legs work, moving towards him. 'The answer to what prayers?'

'You were so good with her. So good for her. I thought— I thought you were a miracle-worker, but you're just as selfish as her mother.'

Paige sucked in a sharp breath, her fingertips itching and then, before she could realise what she was doing, before she could stop herself, her hand lifted and struck his cheek, the slap loud even against the backdrop of the storm. Rain fell, drenching them, and they stared at each other, both shocked by what she'd done. His cheek changed colour, dark pink, and Paige's hand stung. She pulled back, disgusted by herself, by what she'd allow herself to become, but she couldn't apologise. She was too hurt, too angry.

'You don't know anything about me,' she said quietly to herself, as a defensive mechanism, self-protective, because she didn't want his charge to be true. She was putting herself first, though. Above him, and above Amanda, but only because she knew that if she didn't, the loss would be impossible to bear. She would wither away if she didn't go now.

'I hate you,' she said, surprised how satisfying that felt to say, when the truth was she loved him. Even then, in the midst of this, she loved him in a life-altering way, but she also hated him for what he was saying and for how he was reacting.

'I think that's mutual.'

Paige's gut churned. Her words had been thrown out carelessly, seeking satisfaction, but Max's? His, she believed.

She turned to face him, glad that it was pouring with rain, that she was saturated, glad because her tears were disguised by the raindrops. Only they weren't disguised, not really. Her eyes were a perfect mirror to her sadness and shock, showing anyone who would look at her just how she was feeling.

Max though didn't soften.

'Pack your things. Reg will take you to the airstrip.'

She stared at him.

'What?' The word was dredged up from deep inside her chest.

'You heard me. Go,' he shouted, pointing to the house.

She shook her head, lifting a hand to her lips to silence the sobs. 'I want to stay the week. I want to break this to Amanda. To say goodbye properly. To cook with her again, and explain—'

'Do not stand there and act as if you give a flying— anything about her. She's my daughter, and I'll look after her, just like I always have.' His features were like iron. She sobbed audibly now. 'Go!' he said again, voice rich with command and fury.

With her heart in shreds, Paige did exactly that, spinning on her heel and running back to the house, running so fast her feet kicked mud up against her legs, running, crying, utterly destroyed.

He shouted a curse word into the forest, closing his eyes as the last ten minutes replayed in his mind like some kind of horror movie. He'd set something in motion by coming out here when he was so angry, but he was still too angry to see that there was any alternative, to contemplate how to fix this. All he wanted was for Paige to go so he could concentrate on getting the hell on with his life. Without her.

The storm cleared in time for Paige's flight to take off, as if the same hand of fate that had brought her here to Max was also paving the way for her to leave, perhaps realising that their magnetic poles really didn't mix after all.

She stared out of the window of the light aeroplane at all of the things she'd come to love in her time here, at the scorched, orange desert now rendered dark brown by the rain, at the almost ethereal trees, dried out on the side of the dirt-track roads, no leaves, no life, and she felt a strange sympathy for them, a kinship, because she was sure that if there was a way to peer inside her soul, that was exactly what it would look like right now.

Withered, empty, lifeless.

* * *

'What do you mean, she had to go?' Amanda's face showed confusion.

Max wanted this day to be over.

He wanted to wash his hands of it completely.

Paige was still in the air of the house. If he closed his eyes he could smell her, see her. He half expected her to come walking through a doorway at any point, her beautiful smile, her sparkling eyes… His gut tightened.

She was gone. He'd made sure of that.

And what alternative had there been?

Let her stay until it suited her to leave?

Just roll over and have it all on her terms?

No.

It was just him and Amanda, like always. The two of them. He wasn't sure why he'd let himself start to see Paige as part of their team, but at some point, he had. It was a mistake.

She was a temporary fixture in their lives and whether she stayed three weeks or three months, it didn't matter to him.

He repeated that to himself silently, sure that eventually it would ring true.

'Dad? You're kidding, right?'

'No, honey.'

'Dad?'

Amanda pushed her chair back, staring at him with teary blue eyes. His gut rolled, and rather than admitting how much he understood Amanda's feelings, he felt his anger surge. Paige had done this. She was supposed to fix things and instead she'd come and messed it all up even worse.

'I don't want her to go. I wanted her to stay.'

'She was never going to stay for ever, you know that. Paige just came to help out a bit.'

'And she was helping,' Amanda cried. 'I liked her. I loved her. She was so fun, and kind, and when I hugged her, I just felt—like everything was okay again. How could you do this?'

He felt as if he'd been punched. Not just because of the accusation but because of the way she'd perfectly articulated her feelings for Paige, and the way they somehow resonated with his own.

'It was her decision.'

'She would *never* leave without saying goodbye to me. I know her.'

He grimaced. His daughter was right; her faith in Paige was worthy. Paige had wanted to stay, to do this better, properly, maybe in a way that would have avoided Amanda experiencing this pain, but he'd forced her to leave earlier. For his own sake.

Who exactly was the selfish one?

He ground his teeth.

'There is no sense discussing this further.' His words were unnecessarily abrupt. He stood, moving into the kitchen and bracing his palms against the counter. 'She's gone. We'll be fine without her. Fine.'

'I don't want—'

He didn't want either, but it hadn't been his choice.

'Go to your room, Amanda.' The response was sharper than he'd intended. 'You must have homework to do.'

She shoved her chair into the table, stalked to the door. 'I hate you!'

He closed his eyes, despair a fog that was seeping into

his cells. He was two for two, then, in both the most important conversations of his day. Just bloody brilliant.

'I knew she wouldn't leave without saying goodbye,' Amanda shouted victoriously, ten minutes later, stalking back into the kitchen and slamming a piece of paper down in front of him.

Max was standing exactly where he had been when Amanda left the room.

It took him a moment to focus his attention on the page.

Dearest Amanda,

Darling girl, it breaks my heart to leave you; I'm so sorry.

I came to Wattle Bay thinking I was just accepting another job, that you would just be another child, but you're not. You are so special, Amanda, and you are so very special to me. I have adored spending time with you, and I'll always be grateful for how you opened up to me. You are so brave.

I'm sorry to leave you. Please know that while I won't physically be here, my heart remains in this magical, amazing place. I might be on the other side of the world, but you will be in my thoughts always.

Any time you want to speak to me, you can call.
With all my love,
Paige X

She'd included a phone number at the bottom of the letter. There were also a couple of smudge marks to the ink. Tears?

Max found it hard to breathe. And then it occurred to

him that if she'd left a note for Amanda, maybe, just maybe, she'd left a similar message for Max? Something to explain…to tell him… 'Where did you get this?'

'She left it on my desk.'

He stalked out of the kitchen without another word, down the corridor to his study, into his office, where he wrenched open the door, looked around and then slumped his shoulders.

There was no note for him, but what would such a letter say, in any event?

They'd spoken all the words, out in the forest, and those words had been brutal and eviscerating. From him.

'You're just as selfish as her mother.'

Was it any wonder Paige hadn't left a lovely little good-bye note in here for Max?

He groaned, pressed his palm to his forehead and tried to settle the feeling that he'd set the world spinning in completely the wrong direction.

Amanda had left the note on the bench and gone back to her room so when Max returned to the kitchen, he lifted it and reread it, more slowly this time. Certain sentences required him to read them a few times over.

It breaks my heart to leave you.

She'd promised her heart wouldn't break. That her heart didn't get involved when she was on a job. Did she mean what she'd written to Amanda? Or was she just trying to soften the blow to a vulnerable kid?

You are so brave.

He couldn't say why, but those words lodged in his brain, making something shift, something change, so he found it hard to think of that sentence without feeling a thousand and one things for Paige.

Please know that while I won't physically be here, my heart remains in this magical, amazing place.

He read that sentence many times.

Was that true?

It was like staring into murky water. He couldn't see a damned thing and didn't even know what he was looking for, but he knew he wanted the water to clear; he wanted to understand.

He drove himself half crazy that night, memorising the letter and listening to it in his mind, hearing it as though Paige were reading it, and as he fell asleep he imagined that the letter had been written to him, and not Amanda. It was a stupid, indulgent form of torture and he should have known better.

CHAPTER THIRTEEN

PAIGE HAD ENOUGH savings to take some time off. Not a lot, and she couldn't live luxuriously, but she could buy herself a bit of breathing room, rack up her credit card a little if necessary. She could take a break.

And that was exactly what she needed—something to stave off the constant sense of weariness. Only, in not working, Paige lacked occupation and purpose and, rather than having a reason to get out of bed each morning and face the long, lonely day, she found herself dithering, the days blending into each other, all as pointless as the next, everything lacking importance and urgency.

At least Sydney was a beautiful place to wait out her heartbreak—she could acknowledge freely that, yes, her heart was indeed splitting apart. Leaving Max and Amanda had been much, much harder than leaving her parents, than facing their betrayal. That had taken years and she'd had so many examples to look at to justify why she had to get out.

With Max, everything had been so perfect, except for how she'd fallen in love with him.

But then, there'd been that last day, and the way he'd acted, and the things he'd said, and she couldn't remember that fight without feeling as if she was going to fall over. It had been so awful. For his face to contort with anger and that anger to be directed at her!

Ten days after leaving the farm, she had no idea if she'd ever be able to put him from her mind, if she'd ever wake up without wanting to reach for him, without wanting to run to the kitchen to wait for him to appear. Without wanting to hug Amanda and cook dinner with her. Without feeling she'd briefly belonged to a family, even if that was just a fantasy in her head and heart. It had been the closest thing to a family she'd ever known.

Paige didn't realise she was crying until the tears splashed onto the backs of her hands, clasped in her lap. She stared at them, not surprised, not reacting, not bothering to wipe away the tears. They were par for the course these days. They would pass, just like the storm on that last day in Wattle Bay. But the feeling of loss would always be a part of Paige. At least it was something to hold onto, a reminder that yes, one time, she had loved, so deeply, she had known for certain that she was changed.

She'd been brought back to life—no matter how painful it was.

He hated himself for it, but in the end he bought her parents' damned tell-all book. He bought it because, after two weeks of missing Paige like a limb, he was desperate for *anything* remotely connected to her, and too proud to use the number she'd left Amanda and just call her.

Besides, what would he say? What had changed since she left? Nothing.

She'd run away. He didn't know why, but she'd left. He couldn't have changed her mind: he'd tried. Okay, admittedly not very well, but he'd made it obvious he wanted her to stay. She'd wanted to leave, more than she'd been willing to listen, and so he'd made her leave.

But just remembering the way her shoulders had sagged and her face had fallen when he'd shouted at her to go made shame swirl through him.

With a glass of earthy red wine on the table and Amanda asleep for the night, he began the gruesome job of reading the book written by her parents. Page by page, story by story, year by year of young Paige's life, he read about the woman he'd come to know, and it was like having the gaps of his understanding filled in. Not by the stories in the book. He wasn't sure they were accurate, nor was he sure they had any merit in the telling, but in the way her parents wrote about her, in what *wasn't* on the page, he came to understand more about Paige than he had before.

He came to understand what she'd been through, what it must have been like to be raised—no, not raised, so much as exploited—by people like this. People who were still trying to exploit her. In their stories, cynically told to paint Paige in the least flattering light possible, he saw through that, all the way to the heart of a warrior, of a girl who'd been rendered so vulnerable by her life's circumstances, but who'd fought back. How she'd fought back! That she was so strong and wise and capable was completely beyond belief. That she was capable of love, as she professed to love Amanda?

Remarkable.

He read the book through the night, until the dawn light filtered through the kitchen and the day awakened, fresh and golden, right as a different kind of awakening moved through Max. A fresh perspective.

An understanding, finally.

Now as he replayed their time together, and particularly that last day, his comprehension was less certain, his own anger far less justifiable. His selfish stupidity completely unforgivable. But that didn't mean he was above asking for forgiveness.

If he knew anything now, it was that miracles were possible—you just had to be smart enough not to screw them up.

Paige didn't move when the knock came at the door.

She didn't know anyone in Sydney, and she didn't want any room service or any other kind of interruption. She wanted the world to go away.

She shifted on the sofa, lifting her feet up and pressing her chin to her knees, watching the daytime television without really seeing what was on. Some medical drama with far too much angst for Paige to enjoy it, but then again, she was hardly paying attention. It was just background noise as she tried to thaw out from the numbing of all her feelings and senses.

The knock came again, more imperative and demanding, an open-palmed punch almost. She flinched, turned the TV down.

'Go away, please,' she called out. Then muttered, under her breath, 'I'm not interested.'

'I need to talk to you, Paige.'

She froze, her heart in her throat, as the voice she'd been hearing in her dreams flooded her mind, made the hairs on the back of her neck stand on end, made everything hum as if with electricity.

It *couldn't* be Max.

She was imagining it.

It was her mind, playing tricks on her. She stood only because she needed confirmation of her insanity—maybe a hospital was a better place for her? She needed to know just how bad things were for her to conjure him up like this.

At the door, she hesitated just long enough to pull her hair over one shoulder—she couldn't remember the last time she'd washed it but thanked God she'd had a shower that morning and actually put on a fresh outfit.

Not that he was really here, she told herself sternly, wrenching in the door and expecting to see clear air.

But instead, she was confronted by the sight of Max, the same but different. Facial hair was longer, face was pale, eyes had a smudge of darkness beneath them. He looked as exhausted as she felt.

'Max?' Was it really him?

'I need to talk to you.'

She blinked at him, frowning, not understanding. In a monumental effort, she summoned every protective mechanism she'd built in her lifetime, wrapping herself in a shield, quickly trying to fortify her heart and soul. 'What? Why? Is it about Amanda?'

'No. Not directly.' His Adam's apple jerked as he swallowed. 'Can I come in?'

She shook her head instinctively. Memories were too intense, too strong. The power he wielded to hurt her was terrifying.

'Please.' He put a hand on the edge of the door frame,

looking past her, a hint of desperation in his face. 'Just give me a few minutes.'

She shook her head again. Apart from anything, the tiny apartment she'd rented for the next few weeks was a mess, courtesy of the complete lack of a care she'd been capable of giving since flying into the city.

'You can't come in,' she said throatily. 'But there's a cafe around the corner. We can go and grab a coffee.'

He breathed out slowly. 'Great. That will be great. Thank you.'

So polite! Such a startling contrast to the day on the edge of the forest. She spun away from him blindly, moving back into the apartment, tears sheening her eyes. Her emotions were rioting all over the place.

'I'll just get my keys,' she mumbled.

'I'm sorry, what did you say?' Damn it, he'd followed her, he was right behind her, and the door swung softly closed, leaving them alone in the small, unimpressive space. His eyes flicked across the room, sizing it up in a few short seconds, then returned to Paige's face.

'Paige...' His voice was so gravelled and hoarse. 'Why did you leave us?'

It wasn't fair for him to be here! Not after two weeks. 'I can't—' She sucked in a breath, trying to calm her nerves. 'I can't talk about this here.' She needed the safety of others, of crowds, of strangers.

A muscle jerked in his jaw. He moved closer and she stiffened, terrified that he'd touch her and she'd combust. That her self-restraint and pride would fly out of the window.

'Don't.' She held up a hand, closed her eyes. 'Please don't.' She shook her head. 'How did you find me?'

'The agency.'

She lifted her brows, eyes pinging open. 'They're not supposed to give out our addresses.'

'I told them you'd left something personal I needed to get back to you.'

'You lied?' She shook her head. 'Why?'

'I don't consider it to be a lie. Paige, I want you to come home.'

Home.

The word was like a dagger to her heart. She spun away from him, staggering into the living room, sitting down because she wasn't sure she could stay standing.

'Listen to me.' He came to crouch in front of her. 'Listen to me, all of me, everything I say, before you react. Do you promise?'

She didn't think he was in any position to be asking her to promise anything, but she nodded because she wanted to hear whatever he'd come to say, and she needed some time to strengthen her nerves before she asked him to leave. *Go.* She shuddered as she remembered the way he'd ordered her out of his life. Her chin tilted defiantly as she did everything she could to stay strong against him, against his closeness.

So she nodded, and then, when he frowned, she wondered if he'd really expected her to agree, because he seemed momentarily lost, distracted, his eyes simply clinging to her face as if he'd never seen her before. She wore no make-up, she'd barely slept. Self-consciously, she wiped her cheeks and that seemed to pull him from his reverie.

'I miss you.'

She sobbed, tilting her face away. This was just too cruel.

'I miss you, every second of every minute of every hour of every day. I wake up looking for you, wanting you, needing you, looking forward to spending time with you, to being with you, to showing you places and things and experiencing them through your eyes, and then, when I realise you're gone, it's like losing you all over again, it's like reliving that awful fight we had, it's like walking through my very worst nightmare. When you came to the farm, I thought you'd be a temporary employee, someone who'd slot into our lives and then leave again without any difficulty. I couldn't *wait* for you to go, before you'd arrived, because I viewed the hiring of a nanny as a necessary evil. I didn't want to repeat the mistakes of my father. But you were nothing like I imagined. Nothing like I could have prepared for. You're not like anyone I've ever met.'

Another sob. She blinked away.

'Did you leave because you were scared of how much you were coming to care for us, Paige?'

Her tortured, aching heart. It was too broken. She didn't have the strength to lie, and so she lifted her head in a half-nod, her eyes boring into his, daring him to hurt her with that information.

'Because you were falling in love with me after all?'

Her throat hurt from the effort of not crying.

'Please stop this.'

He put a hand on her knee though, a gentle, sensitive hand, and her insides trembled.

'I read your parents' book.'

'What?' It was a plaintive whisper. Tears streamed down her cheeks. 'Why?'

'Because I missed you,' he said honestly. 'I was so desperate for anything of you, anything. I couldn't just call you after the way I'd spoken to you, I didn't even have a photo of you. So I bought the book and I read it last night.'

She closed her eyes. 'I don't want to hear about it. I've been avoiding the whole thing, you know that.'

'I do.' His other hand shifted to her cheek, gentle and caring. 'Paige, what you went through with those people...'

She jerked away from him, standing, trembling, moving to the small, grimy window that looked out onto a multi-storey car park. 'I don't need to hear this,' she said with a valiant attempt at strength. 'I lived it once.'

'I know. And you told me. You told me how awful they were and how you had to divorce them and I didn't get it. It wasn't until I read the book that I really understood what your childhood was like, and what an incredible, unique, brave, giving person you are. That for you to have come through that, to have emerged with such strength and dignity, to have had the courage to write the life for yourself that *you* wanted, that you have had the ability to love at all, after that, I was blown away. You fell in love with Amanda. I know you did, because she showed me the letter.' He was silent. 'I think you fell in love with me too. I think you fell in love with me and you were so scared that I wouldn't love you back, that you left. Am I right?'

She closed her eyes, hating that he'd worked this out, hating how stupid she must seem to him. He was being so nice about it all, but Paige was mortified.

'So what?' she asked, spinning around and staring at him, hardly seeing through her tears. 'What good does it do to come here and have this conversation? Are you so desperate to understand that you'd really make me admit this to you now?'

'Can you really not see?'

She *couldn't* see. Not literally or metaphorically.

'Paige, you are the only lightning I've ever felt in my life. I have never known anything like this. You think that didn't scare me to hell too? I was so scared I didn't even admit the truth to myself until a few hours ago. But God, Paige, I love you. You have taught me the true meaning of love, you have been the answer to questions I didn't even know I had. You are a piece of me that has been missing all my life. That day in the forest, I was so angry I was almost out of my body. Even as we were arguing, I was shouting at myself to shut up and calm down, to stop ruining everything, but I couldn't, because I was standing on the precipice of the greatest loss of my life and I couldn't bear to lose you, Paige. I can't bear to lose you again.'

'I don't believe this,' she sobbed, but a different sob now, one of confusion and wonder. Was he being serious?

'Really?' He held his palms wide. 'Look at me. Just look. I have come here with more desperate longing and hope than any man has ever felt.'

'What do you want?' she whispered, still cautious.

'You were brave enough to fall in love with me. What I want to know is are you brave enough to live in that love? To let it be a part of you, your daily life, every day, for the rest of our lives?'

She gasped, shaking her head, because it was way too much. Way more than she could ever have hoped for. That he loved her was one thing, but that he wanted to marry her? Was that what he meant?

'Yes, damn it,' he said on a tortured groan, and Paige realised she'd spoken the question aloud. 'I want to marry you. I want to marry you two weeks ago, I want to marry you ten years ago. You are the missing part of me and now that I see that, I never want to miss you again. You're my family, Paige, our family. Amanda and I both miss you. We want you to come home. To *our* home, where you belong, where you'll always, always belong. Please.'

His voice was so rich with emotions, too many emotions for Paige to doubt his sincerity. She felt it radiating through her, seeping into her pores first, then her blood, and, finally, her heart, leaving no room for worry.

She nodded once and it was enough. Max strode the short distance across the room and lifted her up, arms wrapped around her middle, kissing her through salty tears, holding her tight to his body, holding her right where he intended for her to be for the rest of their days.

EPILOGUE

SUNSETS OVER THE beach were one of Paige's favourite things. It was strange, she supposed, that the ending of the day could make her think of new beginnings but it did, for dawn was an implicit promise in the going down of the sun. Or perhaps it was that here, in Australia, the colours were different from anything else she'd known before.

Two years after her parents' book was published, Paige could honestly say she barely thought of them. There were times when she was reflecting on her own family—married to Max, and a much-loved stepmother to Amanda—when Paige wished she had a better parenting model to base her own decisions on, but in those moments Max would simply remind Paige to follow her instincts. Her instincts, he told her, were always good.

And perhaps they were.

It had been instinctive to come to Australia. To be brave and let herself love Max even when that terrified her. To return here with him, quite simply, to come home.

And it was home: this tree house on the edge of the continent, with the ocean lapping at the cliffs beneath them. Two years after that awful time in her life, Paige could honestly say she'd never been happier.

Amanda met Paige's eyes in the mirror and grinned. At thirteen, Amanda was a beautiful, funny, smart and confident teen. While she had the occasional emotional outburst, it was abundantly clear that having Paige in her life had been good for the girl. They loved one another very much, and Amanda's friendship issues had settled down too, so sleepovers in the attic of their house had become a regular occurrence for Amanda and her friends.

'Are you ready?' Paige asked.

'Oh, yes.'

'You're sure this isn't too much?' Paige gestured to Amanda's outfit.

Amanda's grin widened. 'Don't lose your nerve now.'

Paige laughed. 'Okay, okay. Well, let's do this quickly, before your aunt and uncle arrive.'

Though they were happily ensconced in their life in Sicily, Mia and Luca were regular visitors to Australia, and their children had become a staple for Paige, Amanda and Max. Neither Mia nor Paige had ever had a sister, and yet they'd become that to one another, almost immediately.

Paige had given herself over to the idea of loving without limits—once she'd started, she'd found she couldn't stop, anyway—and in exchange, she'd received an abundance of love. From Luca, Mia, and their beautiful children—now her nieces and nephews. Her heart was full. While in an ideal world it would be the parents who loved and doted on a person, there was no guarantee this would be the case, and Paige, unable to change her past, simply accepted with gratitude the happiness of her present.

Downstairs, Max was putting the finishing touches on dinner. The sun was low on the horizon, bathing the kitchen in a golden light. Nerves filled Paige's tummy with but-terflies, but when Max turned and smiled at her, they dis-sipated. Everything was okay. Better than okay.

'Max,' she said, reaching for an ice-cold glass of water and taking a sip. 'I bought a new shirt for Amanda. I... hope you like it.'

A frown briefly flickered on his face. 'If you bought it, I'm sure I will.'

'I hope so.'

He arched a brow then turned as Amanda entered the kitchen. The shirt itself was oversized and a crisp white, so Max shrugged. 'It's nice.'

Paige nodded thoughtfully, nervous once more. 'Why don't you spin around, honey?'

Amanda's grin was pure cheek as she did what Paige suggested, so the back of the shirt came into view.

Big Sister—Coming Soon.

Max read the words without comprehending and then, a moment later, turned to Paige, jaw dropping. 'Does that— is that just the design of the shirt?' His voice was hoarse, thickened by emotion.

Paige shook her head.

'You mean—we're having a baby?' He looked from Paige to Amanda, a thousand emotions rushing through him. The last time he'd found out he was going to be a par-ent, it had been an incredibly conflicted time. He'd loved the idea of Amanda from the start, and had known he'd do anything and everything to protect her, but being tied to Lauren was not something he'd relished. Whereas, the idea of their family welcoming another baby, a baby that he and Paige had made together out of the deepest form of love...

'Say something,' Paige demanded, tilting her head back, so he was jolted into action, wrapping her into a big hug, holding her tight, his eyes meeting Amanda's over Paige's head. Their daughter was smiling, looking at them from a couple of metres away, and though Paige couldn't see Amanda, she held out her hand, reaching for her, so Amanda joined them in the hug, their family, the most precious people in his world.

He was so happy he could hardly bear it.

Much later, after the Cavallaros had left and Amanda was in bed upstairs, Paige settled herself on Max's lap, out on the veranda, a beatific smile on her face.

'You, my darling wife, are an excellent secret-keeper. How long have you known?'

'Only a week,' she said, snuggling in close to him.

He let out a low whistle. 'A week!'

'I know. I wanted to tell you, it was so hard not to, but then I accidentally let it slip to Amanda and she came up with this idea—how could I say no?'

He shook his head, arms wrapped around his wife. 'You couldn't, and I'm glad. It feels right that she was a part of announcing it, not just to me but to Luc and Mia too.'

'That's exactly how I felt. I wanted Amanda to know that this is our news, not just yours and mine, but hers too. I never want her to feel excluded.'

He kissed the top of Paige's head. 'You are so thoughtful. Have I told you today how much I love you?'

She laughed, because these were words Max spoke often. 'Nope,' she lied, because she loved hearing it.

'Ah.' He grinned. 'How remiss of me. Then let me tell

you, my darling, beautiful Mrs Stone, that you are my everything, and always will be.' He pressed a hand to her flat stomach. 'I cannot wait to meet the baby we have made together.'

Wait he did though, another seven months, and then, on a balmy, starlit night, at a hospital in the nearest city, in a fast and smooth delivery, Paige propelled their son from her body, clutching the little boy with his shock of dark hair to her chest. Love exploded through her—she felt it when she looked at Max, Amanda, and now their baby, the beautiful little boy that they named Everett, meaning strong, because he was every bit as strong as his parents.

Another baby followed within the next eighteen months, and, with their family complete, they found themselves spending most holidays and birthdays with the Cavallaros, whether in Italy or Australia, or Singapore, or France, or wherever the wind blew them. Paige no longer felt she had to hide from her past, from the fame that had been thrust upon her. It was a part of her history, her life, but it did not define her: she was her own woman, and her life was hers to curate and create, to fill with the people she loved, who loved her back fiercely, determinedly, and always would.

* * * * *

Did you fall head over heels for
Contracted and Claimed by the Boss?
Then you're sure to adore the first installment in the
Brooding Billionaire Brothers duet
The Sicilian's Deal For "I Do"

And be sure to check out these other
Clare Connelly stories!

Pregnant Princess in Manhattan
The Secret She Must Tell the Spaniard
Desert King's Forbidden Temptation
The Boss's Forbidden Assistant
Twelve Nights in the Prince's Bed

Available now!